Return to Shirley Plantation: A Civil War Romance

By
Carrie Fancett Pagels

Hearts Overcoming Press

Second Edition

January 2016

Hearts Overcoming Press

ISBN-13 978-0-9971908-0-9

Cover Art by Roseanna M. White

Dedication

This book is dedicated to Julian Charity and Kathy Maher, without whom this story could not have come to life as it did!

Carrie Fancett Pagels

Chapter 1

Southern Ohio, 1862

Matthew Scott basked in accomplishment's warmth as the theater emptied. Every seat had been filled, save one—Father's. A congressman for their locale, Theodore Scott departed earlier to an emergency meeting with a colleague in Dayton.

Having toiled unceasingly for his troupe to remain together despite the war, Matthew complained only of difficulty with wardrobe. Two gowns already had side seam tears. His face tightened—the seamstress who'd contracted to sew the clothing had failed to arrive the previous year. They'd farmed the work out to a tailor already over-burdened.

Scott's Theatrical Troupe was booked through the next three months for stops in cities and some to entertain the Northern troops. He grinned. Nearby, thespian J. W. Booth pulled on gloves, tipped his top hat at Matthew and exited the building. Matthew retrieved his beaver hat from its peg and followed suit.

Outside, the last of the carriages clustering the circle departed.

"Mr. Scott?" Cigar smoke accompanied the deep Southern-accented voice.

Matthew waited for his eyes to adjust from the interior light to night's velvet blackness.

"Yes?"

"You're coming with us."

Shirley Plantation, Charles City Virginia June 1862

Angelina Rose carried the heavy tray of hot tea, biscuits, honey, porcelain cups and saucers, and silver spoons to a cherry sideboard. The Carter women gathered in the parlor for Bible study.

"Lou, will you read first, dear?" Mary Braxton Carter, matron of Shirley Plantation directed her request to her daughter-in-law.

Louisa, the wife of Robert Randolph Carter, off serving in the Navy, sat up straight. "Matthew 25, verse 34 to begin. 'Then shall the King say unto them on his right hand, Come, ye blessed of my Father, inherit the kingdom prepared for you from the foundation of the world: For I was an hungred, and ye gave me meat: I was thirsty, and ye gave me drink: I was a stranger, and ye took me in: Naked, and ye clothed me: I was sick, and ye visited me: I was in prison, and ye came unto me.'"

Angelina poured each woman a steaming cup of bohea. She mixed in a half-teaspoonful of honey for Louisa and a full spoonful for Fanny—then she added three cubes of sugar for their mother-in-law. She used silver tongs to lay a biscuit on each china plate and pressed a pat of butter atop each. She daren't let anything touch her skin—mixed race skin, being one eighth African. And though no longer a slave, but a free woman, she was a servant in this household. Granted, her original hire was for seamstress chores. But with the war, Angelina had assumed some duties in the house.

Mary B. gestured toward the settee. Nearby, Angelina's nephew and niece sat—Charity's legs tucked beneath her, and Julian's folded, on the wool carpet.

Angelina pressed her hands together in her lap, rumpling her apron. If she took the children and fled for the north, would strangers take them in? Comfort them? The Bible verses promised so. Yet she'd not believed it over a year earlier when she'd declined Mary B.'s offer to set her up as a seamstress in the north. She'd not been able to bear the thought of being separated from the children—her only family.

Fanny, another Carter daughter-in-law, took her turn reading more verses. "Then shall the righteous answer him, saying, Lord, when saw we thee an hungred, and fed *thee*? or thirsty, and gave *thee* drink? When saw we thee a stranger, and took *thee* in? or naked, and clothed *thee*?"

Finally finished with her duties, Angelina lowered herself onto the settee, careful not to allow her skirts to brush against Louisa's.

"Angie, it's your turn." Louisa handed her the Bible.

Although her benefactress in Richmond had taught her to read, Angelina detested doing so aloud. But looking into little Charity's eyes, she couldn't decline—her niece needed to hear these words as well. Julian stood and looked over her shoulder.

Angelina's neck perspired. "Or when...saw we thee sick, or in prison, and came unto thee?"

"So we're 'sposed to go to everybody and check on them like Mrs. Carter does?" Julian aimed his gap-toothed grin at the matron.

"Yes, Julian—and others. And comfort those held captive." Her face crinkled. "As I pray some kind northern woman will do for my boys, should something ever befall them."

Sensing Mrs. Carter on the verge of tears, Angelina continued on, her hands shaking beneath the heavy tome. "And the King shall answer and say unto them, Verily I say unto you, Inasmuch as ye have done *it* unto one of the least of these my brethren, ye have done *it* unto me."

After wiping her eyes with an embroidered handkerchief, Mrs. Carter rose from the brocade settee. Her daughters-in-law filtered out of the room, but she placed a restraining hand on Angelina.

"I didn't want to tell the girls." Those so-called girls were grown women with families of their own. "But there's much military activity not far from here."

Everyone knew of the peninsula campaign. So why the concern? Perhaps because McClellan's gunboats sat in the James River in full view of Shirley Plantation, something that had caused great excitement down in the slave quarters.

Tiny pearl-like teeth nibbled on Mary B's lower lip. "I'd prefer you and your sister's children to take a room in the Old House. I don't want you to continue to sleep over the laundry."

Energy siphoned away from Angelina. She'd not be able to transport her sewing machine by herself. The lower floor had been converted back to laundry work after having been used as a school when Robert E. Lee lived at Shirley with his mother. Long before her sister Lorena had been sold to the Carters.

Angelina glanced around the graciously appointed room, ensuring no one would overhear them. "Mrs. Carter, I hoped my earnings from my private work last month could pay off Julian's and Charity's expenses." Could she leave with the Union army?

Mary B.'s blue eyes blinked rapidly. "You don't understand. The armies are moving our way. They'll likely destroy or occupy all the farms in Charles City County, including this one. We must pray, dear, pray very hard. Pray for God's will."

"Yes'm." She'd been a fool to stay behind when she could have gone north with her freedom papers. She could have earned the money through her sewing contract with the theater company to have brought the children north.

"I'm sorry my husband didn't free the children and let them leave with you for Ohio—he was too preoccupied with war and what he perceives as his duty to the commonwealth." She ran a hand over an elaborately engraved 17th century sterling English covered serving dish.

Angelina had already begun packing their meager belongings above the laundry to flee, despite the sensation that God was telling her to stay. Yet when she'd heard the scripture verses now, she'd wondered if they were meant for her—to trust and go. Niggling doubt wrestled with the sensation that something important was held in those words for her.

Patting both children's shoulders she then rose. "We'll go get our things, won't we, children?"

Charity's auburn head bobbed and Julian's green eyes lit. "Come up here to the Great House?"

"To the Flanker House. And hurry—it's almost nightfall." Granny Scott, the oldest slave at Shirley, sometimes filled the children's heads full of superstitions to the point where they'd become frightened to be out at dark. Something Angelina hoped to overcome through a steady application of the Bible.

Malvern Hill. Virginia.

War.

Matthew had landed in hell, where a cacophony of noise thundered around him. And before he fell to the ground of the battlefield, he watched himself raise his rifle and fire upon a line of blue-coated soldiers. *God forgive me.* Then the velvet curtain of blackness separated him from consciousness and his audience.

Matthew raised his throbbing head. Where was he? He inhaled the scent of death, and passed out again. Waking later, the sun setting, he spied gray uniformed bodies surrounding him in the dirt. Twenty-five days he'd served with the Confederate army. Sergeant Smith and a band of his men had taken Matthew, son of a Copperhead congressman, and conscripted him. Because of Father's political beliefs, the Union army completely ignored their foray into southern Ohio. Smith said both Father and his crony were taken into custody by the Union army and Matthew could expect no relief from them. How could this happen?

I won't die like this.

The Confederate soldier alongside him, coat coated in blood, turned his light blue gaze upon him. "Guess ya weren't yella, like we thought."

Matthew couldn't remember everything. He recalled forced marches, dirty work, and having a gun shoved in his hand. *Dear God what have I done?*

He lowered his head back to the mucky ground. When he awoke, Confederate Lieutenant Carter groaned beside him "Can you take a letter for me, Scott? I think they'll exchange me but they'll probably take you with them."

The officer, who'd had nothing to do with Matthew's abduction, pressed a missive into Matthew's outstretched hand. "If you get to Shirley, give this to my Mama. Mrs. Mary Braxton Carter."

Blue uniformed Union troops tromped past, pulling men from the field. "We've got to get them out of here."

A Union private pulled Matthew up.

Lieutenant Carter struggled to his feet. "This man is from Ohio and was conscripted into the Confederate army because of his father's political leanings."

Matthew cringed and wished the officer had said nothing. Why would a Union officer be sympathetic to the son of a Copperhead congressman?

A private jerked his thumb at the two of them. "Probably Confederate spies—ought to shoot them, Sergeant Ross."

Peering through his hazy vision at the men, Matthew spied a man with officer's insignia on his shoulder—the one called Ross.

"Get these wounded men out of here as fast you can." He released a string of profanity.

"And swap this one for a Union officer being held by the Rebels."

"Auntie Angie, can I brush your hair?"
Nine-year-old Charity held out a brush as
Angelina sat on a cushioned bench before a
vanity with a real mirror on it—one like she'd
had at the house where she'd lived in
Richmond. Dawn's light streamed through the
two large windows in the room on the first
floor of the flanker building, a building three
stories high but rectangular rather than square
like the Great House.

"Yes, you should learn how to brush
wavy hair, like mine, without tangling it."
Angelina's mass of hair, free from its head
wrap, flowed down to her waist, a cascade of
gold and bronze.

Mama said her papa had blonde hair
straight as a stick and her grandpap before
him. But they were never to talk of either
South Carolinian man, from the plantation
where they'd been born into slavery. Before
she and her sister were sent north to Virginia.
For reasons unknown to her, the mistress of
Rose plantation, a strong Christian woman,
freed Angelina and sent her to live with her
aunt in Richmond, with the stipulation that
she be educated and brought up in the
Christian faith, as well as taught a trade—in
Angelina's case, stitchery and sewing. She'd
served under a French seamstress on Broad
Street, constructing gowns for the fanciest of
occasions, including some held at Shirley

Plantation—where her older sister had been sent.

Lorena, however, hadn't been freed. Her older sister had been slightly darker skinned than Angelina, with chestnut hair and dark eyes. But her children more resembled Angelina. Their father was a fair-haired Charles City feed store proprietor whom her sister had fallen in love with, despite being a slave in the laundry. Her gut wrenched with the stories Lorena had told her of his promises—none kept. But he'd given her these beautiful children, both belonging to the Carters until their freedom could be purchased. Although Mrs. Carter had been apologetic, the best she could provide was the opportunity to go to Ohio and earn a good income—and send for the children later. Something Angelina couldn't bring herself to do.

"I can't believe we're still staying here in the old house." Charity's blue-gray eyes, like her own, reflected in the mirror. "It's been nigh on a week now."

As Charity brushed, Angelina snuck looks at herself in the mirror and at her niece—so sweet like Lorena at that age. Unbidden tears wet her eyes—Charity was worth waiting for as was Julian. Now what, though? Would they be stuck in Virginia for years as this war raged on or were the Shirley

15

men correct—it would all be over in a year? And if it was, would they enact laws which would revert her freed status to slave again? Would she be able to secure papers for the children? Or would they have to journey north as best they could, passing for white. At one eighth African, she and the children should be able to manage. But it was no longer safe to do so. Thinking about her problems only made her head pound. Perhaps she should have gone and sent money back. No—the children would have been separated from her. And she'd clearly heard God telling her to wait.

Unusual noises caught her attention—the sounds of many feet tromping up to the Great House.

"Stop brushing, darlin'." Prickles of fear ran along her scalp where Charity had brushed.

Trodding to the window, she pulled back the velvet curtain then peered through the center crack in the shutters before lifting the S-shaped hook that held them together.

There, covering the entire lawn of Shirley Plantation, was an army. They pitched tents, laid down bedrolls—hundreds of men dressed in blue. The Union Army. Chills chased up her arms. Could they take her north? Unearthly groans carried across the fields to the house.

No one else resided in the Old House, which was falling into disrepair. Costs to fix and replace glass, wood, and brick had become exorbitant once the war had begun. Would the army want to put some of the men in this building?

They'd marched north, the Union army transporting their wounded, but under their watchful eye, Matthew considered. What would it be like to have a wife? Children? Grandmothers and cousins? He'd been told his grandparents were dead, but had found a letter to his father tucked inside his bible. The date on the letter was from one year earlier and in the top corner, his grandmother had written Little River, Kentucky. When he'd asked his mother about the letter, she'd become hysterical, insisting that he had no paternal grandparents.

Why were they dead to her?

They marched alongside the James River, their compatriots making their way down the other side, to set up their own camp. When periodic blackness overtook his vision, Matthew forced his feet to keep moving.

Sergeant Ross rode by. "We're not stopping at Harrison's Landing where McClellan is. We're to continue on."

They'd finally stopped and set up tents at night outside an old colonial plantation—at least a hundred years old from the looks of the brick buildings in the moonlight. At the center stood an impressive square three-story building, two chimneys atop, smokeless on this warm summer night. To the left of it, stood another three-story building, slightly smaller than the center structure and rectangular. The opposite side of the great house was empty, as though it, too, should have a similar building, making a row of three. In front of the houses which stood parallel to the James River, lined double sets of two-story brick edifices, each facing one another across a lawn. He'd never seen anything like it, save in a picture book of an English manor home in the country.

"Matthew, do you have Lt. Carter's letter?" Lieutenant Filmore pulled back the flap to the tent and peered in.

"Yes sir."

"We're on his land. Bring it up to the house. We'll see what these ladies are made of."

What did that mean? "Let me wash up and I'll be right with you."

Now, standing at the top of the steps beneath a large overhang, as Sergeant Ross pounded on the door, a weight settled in Matthew's stomach. Wouldn't his own mother long to hear from him—to know where he was?

Lieutenant Filmore stared at Ross. "Treat these women with respect, men, or you'll answer to me."

Sergeant Ross's mouth twitched beneath his shaggy moustache.

The door creaked open and a tiny woman with salt and pepper hair cocked her head at them.

"Madam, we are taking control of your property…"

A thin hand clutched the chain of a gold cross at her neck. "Come in and tell me what you need."

Coming from the river after washing, Matthew had already observed men scooping up eggs into their hats and bringing them to the cook. Hunks of butter had likewise been retrieved. But the men were hungry and with all the food available on this plantation, he knew it would be pilfered if they were not accommodated.

The matron turned her back to them. The men exchanged glances then followed her into an expansive foyer. The stairs, to the right of the entryway, gave the illusion of hanging in space, for a moment causing Matthew's vision to blur. The room they stood in was as large as some people's homes, with a width of about thirty feet. She looked over her shoulder as she walked beneath an archway.

They followed her to a parlor outfitted with a large fireplace, unlit on this warm June day, the letter in Matthew's pocket nagging to be read.

"Ma'am?" Matthew spoke, despite Ross's glare.

Mrs. Carter turned. He caught the flicker of fear that danced across her face before she put on her "stage face" of benign hospitality.

"I have a letter from one of your sons."

"Praise God. Is he safe?" The tiny woman waited for Matthew to reach her. "Did you see him? Was it Hilly?" She grasped his hands, hers icy cold, revealing her distress— her attempted performance as a calm Southern woman vanished.

Chapter 2

Injured soldiers lay shoulder-to-shoulder as far as Angelina could see, all across the grounds of Shirley Plantation. Someone cooked nearby and she saw a man grinning as he carried a huge shank of bacon to a smoky pit.

Lord have mercy.

A Confederate soldier was marched between two bulky men up the stairs of the Great House. What would they do to him? Was it Hilly? Had he been captured?

Angelina woke Charity. "Honey, you gots to help me dress." She'd slipped into her South Carolinian slave accent that her benefactress had tried to drum out of her.

"Huh?" The girl rubbed her eyes.

"Get up and help me with my corset." Angelina swept her hair up and pinned it. She'd not wear her hair beneath a cloth. She needed to hurry.

"Get me the black dress in the armoire."

Once attired in mourning wear, hoping to discourage any potential masculine interest, Angeline headed to the house, a black veil draped over her face.

She hastened up the front steps and onto the portico. Opening the door, she swept in— as if she belonged. The Carter women had rehearsed this scenario with her.

Mrs. Carter's dulcet tones and a man's bass voice echoed in the center room. Angelina strode through her bombazine skirts to the parlor. *I am not a slave I am a free woman.* A free woman living in the south. The words failed to comfort her.

Upon entry, only one man stood, a man with braid on his shoulders. The Confederate soldier remained seated, a hand resting beneath his chin as he leaned forward. The dark haired man wasn't Hilly. Hazel eyes perused her face. Why did he not rise? A good bath would have further improved the handsome man's looks. But if he got any more good looking…

Her heart performed a somersault that Julian would have been proud of. What was wrong with her? This was a man fighting to keep people like her enslaved.

The man's eyes held intense pain. Why did the Northern officers bring a Confederate soldier into the home?

A tic in Louisa's cheek, beneath her eye, betrayed her fear. "Cousin Angie, come join us. I was just reassuring these gentlemen that we will do our utmost to assist their wounded."

Fanny, Charles Carter's wife, pressed her lips into a tight smile.

"And this young man has a message from one of my sons." Mary B. smiled benevolently first at Angelina and then at the attractive soldier.

"Hilly—is he all right?" Angie's question came out in a rush. The Carter women collectively fixed their eyes on her. She averted her gaze, not wishing to feel Hilly's wife's questioning eyes.

Angelina admired the young man, an ordained minister. He and his mother were two of the reasons she'd decided to remain at Shirley until she could get herself and the children north. Their strong faith had been a constant reassurance. Then the war broke out. And Hilly chose to enlist—surprising her. And truth be told, disappointing her. He was a man of faith, who suffered from epileptic fits, and he'd have been a better source of comfort to his family had he remained home.

"No, ma'am." His voice held a twang unfamiliar to her. He struggled to his feet, swayed slightly then reached inside his coat, retrieving a letter. He offered it to Mary B. and Angelina wished it were her hand that brushed against his as he passed the missive.

Mary B.'s face brightened then fell. "Is he injured?"

"He was, ma'am, but he'll be exchanged for one of our officers."

Matthew licked his dry lips and tried to disengage his vision from the beautiful widow. Despite the black neck-high dress, Angie shone lovelier than any of the other women present—even than any woman he'd ever seen. He pulled his gaze from her blue-gray eyes. Here was a wealthy plantation owner's widow and he'd been disrespectful. Not only that but he was a northerner—a Yankee by their description, though he'd not call himself such. That was a term he'd only heard in reference to New Yorkers and others from the Northeast.

A slender young man entered the room, followed by a distinguished-looking older man, who nodded. "Hill Carter, owner of Shirley Plantation, and this is my son, Dr. Lewis Warrington Carter."

"A physician?" Lieutenant Filmore leaned forward.

"Yes, and I am anxious to help—I see you've many wounded men." Dr. Carter rubbed his chin. "I confess; I awoke to their cries but was unsure if you'd welcome my assistance."

Sergeant Ross snorted. "Shirley is now a field hospital. Of course we can use your help."

Mrs. Carter, her hands clasped demurely, moved silently closer to her son. "Warrington is our eldest surviving child. He studied medicine in Pennsylvania."

"Completed my internship in France."

She smiled up approvingly. "He's our only son at home."

The two men exchanged glances. "I see. I'm not a surgeon but I can care for the men. Do you have supplies?"

"Frankly, we've not been prepared for the great number of casualties, Dr. Carter. Mr. Carter, I am familiar with your name—War of 1812 naval hero I believe."

Hill Carter's lips compressed, his eyes darting among the union men.

"Shame you couldn't convince your sons to fight for America, too." Sergeant Ross smirked and Lieutenant Filmore shot him an icy look.

Mr. Carter remained stock still.

Matthew's respect for Mr. Carter grew as he didn't back down.

"In any event, Mr. Carter, we are now occupying your plantation." Lieutenant Filmore glanced around the well-appointed room. "And will requisition anything we need. Your wife and daughters-in-law have graciously offered to assist."

The beautiful widow's eyes widened. She alone of the women lacked a fan. While the others cooled themselves, she sat upright, still. Why did his eyes continue to be drawn to her? Her hair appeared hastily attended to. Honeyed skin was complemented by rosy cheeks. Or was she blushing? He forced himself to look away.

If he'd been setting up this scene, he'd have had props for each woman, and all would have assistance with wardrobe and stage makeup and hair. Something was seriously amiss...

Sergeant Ross kicked Matthew awake.

"Don't think you fool me with your story—we haven't confirmed what you said. Not that I have any sympathy for the son of a..." Ross launched into a slew of profanity. ... "Copperhead's son."

Despite his headache, Matthew wouldn't be cowed. "Sergeant Ross, I am not my father. I'm the owner of a theatrical troupe."

The bully spit on the ground near Matthew. "I'm keeping an eye on you—and on that pretty gal from the house. I got a feeling about her, too—something's not right."

Other than her being a Confederate soldier's widow? That alone should have been enough to irritate Ross.

"McClellan is at Harrison's Landing." He squinted at Matthew. "If anyone was going to be sympathetic to your story it would be him. But don't count on it. In the meanwhile get your sorry self up and help those women."

Matthew spied the Carter women rolling bandages beneath the rear portico. The back of the house faced the river and boat traffic. Including McClellan's gun boats. What did those ladies think as they toiled there in full view of those guns?

"I'm a strong man." Other than these dizzy spells he now suffered. "I think I can be put to better use."

Now, hours later, Mathew regretted his comment. The Carter women had served the men soup, bread, and weak lemonade as well as performing nursing duties. Meanwhile he'd slapped together ten raised wooden platforms on which the men could be placed and examined.

Movement nearby caught his eye. Angie Carter's competent beauty as she meandered through the field of sick men, stopping to pour water, caused his breath to catch in his chest.

Many of these men wouldn't live past sunset. But at least they'd have some kindness shown them. He swiped a hand at the sweat below his eyes.

One of the soldiers asked her a question. She hesitated and her full pink lips pulled into a narrow line.

Sergeant Ross turned from screaming at a private serving as an orderly and grabbed Angie's upper arm. Matthew stiffened then moved toward the widow.

"Whatever these suffering men require— you're to provide it, do you understand me, Mrs. Carter?" Ross's loud voice carried across the distance as Matthew strode forward.

At first Angelina kept her eyes downcast but when Ross yanked on her arm, she glared up at him.

"Take your hand off me. Now."

Ross averted his gaze to Matthew. His face reddened but he released her arm. He leaned over and whispered something in her ear and the young widow backed away from him, fear flickering over her pretty features.

As Matthew reached her, the sergeant stomped off.

Longing to pull the shaking woman into his arms, Matthew refrained and twisted his cap in his hands. "Mrs. Carter, are you all right?"

Angelina pressed a hand to her chest and strode as quickly as she could, through her heavy false widow's weeds, toward the slave quarters. She stopped at door of the oldest slave on the plantation and tapped gently. Charity and Julian were told to go here if they had any trouble. But now faced with difficulties of her own, Angelina needed comfort. And reassurance that she hadn't made a fool choice by not only staying when she could have gone, but trying to pass as a member of the family.

The door creaked open and the tiny woman opened her arms. "I knew you was comin', Angel."

Unbidden tears flowed down her cheeks as Granny embraced her.

"I gots hominy and some butter that them soldiers didn't swipe. You sit down now." The elderly woman pulled Angelina toward a plain but serviceable table and chairs.

"It's been a long day, Granny."

"Um hum, sure be that. But you young." Halfway through dipping white-gold hominy from the pot and into a small crock for Angelina to eat from, the slave raised her head.

Angelina tipped her head, hearing the faint strains of a trumpet. Some kind of brass instrument, such as she'd heard in orchestras in Richmond. One of the military men she'd nursed had called himself a bugler. He'd praised God that only his left arm was damaged. But would he even live? A tear trailed down her cheek and she brushed it away.

Granny placed the dish atop a strip of cloth that served as a place mat then took Angelina's hand again and led her to the door and outside.

The music floated up from nearby Harrison's Landing.

"That be different music tonight, Angel girl." Tears slid down the woman's face and Angelina's eyes followed suit.

The strain of the bugle call, so poignant, tugged at her heart and the wetness of her cheeks soon matched Granny's.

"They be sad—that why that boy play so forlorn a song." Granny shook her head.

"They lost so many men, Granny." Angelina wrapped an arm around the woman's shoulder.

"Thank you, Jesus, for those boys who died to free us." Her lower lip trembling, the elderly slave tipped her head back, looking up at the darkening sky.

So many dead. So many wounded. So many would yet die.

When the military music ceased sounding from Berkeley Plantation they both returned to the cabin and blotted their faces.

Granny sat in her rocker instead of at the table. "My days comin' to an end soon."

"Don't say that." Angelina's words came out hoarse, hushed.

She laughed gently. "Don't you worry none about me—I knows where I goin' and the angels comin' regular-like to visit me now. Purty near every night."

Dipping a spoon into her hominy, Angelina stirred the mounds round and round in the tiny bowl. "I'm not ready for you to go. You've been so good to me and the children." And to Lorena before she'd died. Angelina blinked back more tears.

"God do everything in His own sweet time. When He say wait—He got a reason. When He say go, He gots His reason then, too."

The creak of the rocking chair, and Granny's words, were enough reassurance for Angelina. She took a bite of the hominy, savoring its buttery taste and rough texture. It tasted of home. What would it be like up north?

Mary B. closed and locked the dining room door. Angelina told her what the vile Sergeant Ross had threatened the previous day. This morning, they'd finished a quick breakfast of ham, biscuits and tea, the same the soldiers would shortly receive—those well enough to eat.

"Not one word today—do you understand me?" The tiny woman shook a finger at them, eying Angelina especially. "Not if you want to keep yourself from harm."

Seated on the floor, the twins hugged closer to Angelina's knees.

"Mama?" Louisa fanned herself vigorously. "I've tried so very hard to hold my tongue."

"Don't you utter one word against the Union men, Lou. I won't tolerate it." Mary B.'s tone was razor sharp.

Fanny's face flushed. "Why not?"

"Hasn't my son told you what one of the Yankee general's has ordered?"

Blinking, Fanny replied, "Charles says political discussions are not for women."

If the topic wasn't so serious, Angelina would have snorted. Numerous times she'd caught Charles's wife hovering near the second floor portico while the men smoked and talked politics. Angelina would clean around her, her feather duster whisking over the furniture as Fanny strained to hear.

Louisa arched her eyebrows. "I've no intention of criticizing these wounded men nor the Union and being labeled a..."

Mrs. Carter's hand shot out to stop the woman. Her soft gaze settled on the children, who gazed up at her. "Well, I'm sure you all understand the peril we're in. But we're Christian, don't forget and we have our duty to God. Let's bow our heads and pray."

As she prayed for them, the groans and shouts of the men carried through the open windows. Unbidden tears rose in Angelina's eyes. How would she make it through another day? She felt in her pocket for the lavender sachet she kept there—a reminder of her sister. She'd need several pomanders today and wished she could make a mask of them. Mary B's fervent prayer lifted Angelina's spirit.

"Amen. All right, I'll organize the slaves—assuming the military hasn't already..."

But Angelina followed Mary B's gaze, swiveling toward the windows.

Sergeant Ross yelled at the field hands and lined them up as though they were his recruits. He was deliberately parading them near the Carter home. They'd already lost a half dozen field hands who'd swam out into the James River and been taken aboard the gunboats. Not that Angelina blamed them.

She'd had a choice. Yet she'd not taken the opportunity and gone. She'd suffered mockery from both the house and kitchen slaves. But old Granny Scott had understood. She'd stroked Angelina's back and told her, "You waitin' on the Lord, Angie; you a good girl to watch over these children."

Mary B., her face more lined today than usual, patted at her plain day dress. "Lou and Fanny, change into something serviceable—then let's be about our mission."

Was this an assignment from God? Perhaps if she served faithfully, there might be some way to go north and take her niece and nephew away to freedom with this army. Angelina stroked their silky hair then patted their shoulders. They'd need to prove useful.

"Come on Charity, you too Julian—we'll not polish anything today but you can let God's love shine through you."

Dimples formed in each child's cheeks.

Julian squared his shoulders. "We'll feed them thirsty and ahungred like it said in the Bible."

Her heart swelled with love. She'd done the right thing in not leaving them. God convicted her of His will. Now would He give her the means to free them?

Sergeant Ross, a scowl on his pock-marked face, marched the field slaves down the rows as though he had new enlistees. What had Matthew done that had merited Ross's unbridled scorn? Perhaps nothing—and the man was simply a tyrant.

Ebony skinned men followed other slaves with complexions more the hue of tanned leather. Women, their heads wrapped in colorful cotton, carried buckets from the well. He drew in a breath when one turned, her appearance and coloration no different than any of the white women walking the streets of his hometown in Ohio. Yet she was a slave. As was the coffee and cream colored woman behind her. Several of the other men nearby also stared.

"I've heard such things but didn't believe it," a private lying nearby muttered. "That's a white woman—pretty as punch, too."

"Keep your eyes in your head, soldier," an orderly advised as he raised the younger man to his feet.

Matthew had seen pictures passed around by Abolitionists, too. And he'd not wanted to consider how such things happened, having been raised to keep his mind focused on what was good, pure, and right. Some surely were born of a loving union. But he was not so naïve as to believe the greater proportion were not.

35

His attention was drawn away as the beautiful Carter widow joined them in the field. Why had she affected him so profoundly? Most men had the good manners to avert their gaze from her widow's weeds—possibly from respect or considering their own wives in such attire. Why couldn't he control his reaction to her?

As a thespian, he urged his troupe to practice and capture facial expressions of the characters they portrayed. This beauty's features, so mobile, spoke of heartache so deep that only a miracle would crack through her defenses to reach and heal her heart. She must have loved her husband deeply. A Confederate soldier. A Southern gentleman. Something Matthew would never be. He wasn't even like his father—someone who was more avoidant than a sympathizer. Or was he?

Angelina grimaced as Sergeant Ross aimed his boot at a soldier with septic wounds, one too near death to even groan.

"Turn him over!" he barked at Phil, one of the field hands.

"Yassah."

"And don't be yassahing me! Refer to me as Sergeant Ross."

"Yassah, Sergeant Ross."

Angelina closed her eyes and bowed her head as Isaiah gently rolled the dying Union soldier over. The inhumanity made her ill. She raised her pomander to her nose and inhaled the fragrance to block the stench, recalling Lorena's death and her sister's plea to not blame the children's father.

He'd left to join the Confederate army instead of running off to the north with her, like he'd promised. As far as Angie was concerned, Lori died of a broken heart.

Lord, accept this man into your hands, and let him die quickly and mercifully, amen.

A hand brushed into her side. She jerked away, thinking it was Ross trying to paw her again. But she looked up into large hazel eyes full of compassion.

"You all right, Mrs. Carter?" His twang, unfamiliar, didn't mark him as a southerner. Perhaps a sympathizer from Kentucky.

The true Mrs. Carter had schooled her in her diction, as had her benefactress, Mrs. Roat, who allowed her to address her as "Aunt Wilda." Angelina now appreciated her stern reminders.

"I was just praying, Private..."

He chewed on his lower lip. "Scott."

"We've a Scott family just one plantation over—Scott's Hundred." And a sweet old slave in the closest cabin, sold off from that plantation long ago.

"Do they send mail from here?" His wide brow furrowed beneath wavy dark hair.

"Why yes, we have the closest dock and mail comes downriver on a steamer for us and several of our neighbors."

"And this address, is it…" A twitch started near his well-formed nose.

"Shirley, Virginia." Why did he ask?

How did Hilly Carter fare? Angelina pressed a hand to Private Scott's arm as she'd observed the Southern belles do when they wanted a favor from a man. "Did you by any chance come across Lt. Hilly Carter in your service?"

"No, ma'am, I did not." A flicker of annoyance crossed his even features but then his eyes slowly scanned her face, lingering on her lips.

She released her hand—suddenly flushed with something not caused by the summer's heat.

"Sorry, Mrs. Carter. Was your cousin very close to you?"

If she didn't know better, she'd think the handsome soldier sounded jealous. And what was she thinking—practically flirting with the man? Fire—she was playing a dangerous game chatting with this fellow. But she couldn't resist.

Chapter 3

Thank God he'd not consumed more of the biscuits the kitchen slaves served as lunch. Matthew reclined on his pallet, and closed his eyes, his head threatening to explode. He'd been fine until he'd encountered the young widow, trailed in her duties by her two sweet children. After their departure, his dizziness increased. *Why Lord, why me? How could you take me from my home, put me in a hostile territory, and allow an injury to my head?*

Someone laid a damp cloth over his forehead and hummed. Matthew drifted into a fitful sleep accompanied by groans and cries. He'd gone to hell, just like he feared he would. A Negro spiritual, one he recognized from childhood, drifted into the cacophony of terror.

"You looks like him, boy." A hand, dry as pork cracklins, brushed his cheek. The humming resumed, soothing.

Sometime later, the air around him seemed to have cooled. Was night already arriving or was he dying? The buzzing inside his head quieted.

"You recollect young Theodocius Scott to me." The voice was aged and low but he was sure he'd heard the slave woman correctly.

How would she know his grandfather's name? Father's, too. And his own middle name?

"Eulalie love that boy somethin' fierce. And he love her too. 'Nuff to take her away from me." The voice recalled the rustling of grass in a gentle breeze.

Eulalie and Theodocius Scott. Matthew tried to shake himself awake. To no avail. He'd seen those names once on a sketch in one of his father's drawers. A man and woman surrounded by a boy and a half dozen girls were drawn seated on a bench in front of a log cabin.

"Granny Scott, what you doin'?" The young widow's voice took on a different cadence.

"I tendin' this boy—he remind me of my Eula's husband." Despite the odor of death, her scent bore traces of cornmeal, ham, and age.

"Granny, he wearin' Confederate clothes." Why did her diction alter?

"I knows, Angel girl, but..."

Matthew opened his eyes and locked on a pair of blue-gray eyes fringed with heavy black lashes.

Mrs. Carter covered her mouth.

He turned his head toward the elderly slave. Her wizened face, the color of chocolate, displayed a serene expression.

"Um hum—he gots them big hazel eyes, too, like I knew he would."

"Granny." Angelina Carter's voice pleaded with the woman.

"President Lincoln come to Berkeley this summer, like the Lord tell me he would. Now this boy here, too." Her smile grew.

Mrs. Carter placed a hand under the slave's arm and pulled her up. "Time for you to get to your cabin—get some rest."

"Yes'm." The woman's large features tightened, then relaxed. "I be back tomorrow."

Sergeant Ross lumbered toward them. "Is that no good Reb still lying around?" He aimed a kick at Matthew but the slave woman stepped between them.

Although Ross slowed the kick, his boot still connected with the stooped woman and she would have fallen had the younger woman not caught her.

"How..." Mrs. Carter's outraged voice suddenly ceased.

Matthew rose and unkinked his stiff body. "Sergeant Ross, your behavior..."

But dressed in his Confederate gray and wobbling, his confidence in his ability to assert any kind of authority wafted away like gunsmoke. He couldn't form his thoughts—other than to protect the widow.

Cigar smoke wafted from nearby. Dr. Probst, a Union surgeon, took Granny by her elbow, bent and examined the frail woman's leg before shooting Ross a scathing look. "They've a saying around these parts, Sergeant—you catch more flies with honey than vinegar."

"I'll get her back to her cabin." Angelina smiled at the physician and then led the elderly woman away.

Matthew's hands itched, longing to pummel Ross.

The scent of tobacco puffed up and then intensified, although it barely covered the stench of decaying flesh. Dr. Probst inhaled a long intake on his pipe. "Sergeant Ross, if I ever catch you again so much as touching your toe to anyone here I will report you. And I shall take delight in removing your marks of rank." He pointed to Ross's uniform.

Ross saluted. "Yes sir. Understood, sir."

"Dismissed."

After he left, the surgeon shook his head. "Someone is going to catch Ross alone one night and he's going to have all those kicks returned. Lord help him."

God save them all. And given Matthew's excellent ability in pugilism, may he restrain himself from delivering Ross's come-uppance.

After she'd dropped off her dress, Angelina stopped by the Old House to retrieve an old petticoat Hilly's wife left there. Much cooler than sitting outside, she sat by a window, shredding cloth into strips for bandages. The floor boards creaked in the hall, although she'd not heard the door open. Dropping the bandages into her lap, she looked up.

Sergeant Ross occupied the parlor doorway. She'd seen the look in Ross's eyes before, one of lust.

Angelina drew a shaky breath. "Are you lost, Sergeant? Or do you require the bandages more urgently?"

A square-built man, he'd lumbered toward her. Her mouth grew dry and she pressed the small of her back against her chair, the wood shield-design seatback jabbing her ribs.

"Thought I saw you, Sergeant Ross." Private Scott strode into the room.

Relief leapt through her.

"What do you want, Scott? I have business to discuss with the lady." His leering eyes as he emphasized the last word left no doubt he considered her no gentlewoman.

Shivering, Angelina wadded the cotton pieces into a ball and shoved them into a pillowcase.

"The lieutenant returned from Berkeley and wants to see you immediately. Colonel Sackett has something to discuss with you."

Hopefully a transfer to Harrison's Landing.

Now, hours later, Angelina's hands still shook. She motioned her niece and nephew outside, awaiting their call to dinner. "Sit here on the stoop with me."

Charity and Julian followed to the front porch of the flanker or "Old House" as the family liked to call it. Generally unused, the past two days she'd swept the first floor and cleaned, falling into bed to sleep like the newly dead, like those she'd discover gone the next morning. At least this way they didn't inhabit her dreams. No—her waking day was a nightmare. Save for the few moments she spent here and there with the very attractive Private Scott.

She rubbed her arms. The Confederate soldier would be horrified to discover she was a freed slave, and the children slaves. Yet she knew her sister's lover didn't fight for the Confederacy because he revered the institution of slavery—he went because he couldn't stand the thought of the North telling Virginians what they could and couldn't do.

What would he do when he discovered Lorena had died?

She patted the step beside her and the children sank down. They, too, had served the injured Union troops, carrying water and mopping brows. Charity sang for some of the men—some of the hymns from their own church and she'd had to pull her away, fearing questioning by someone. Fear, everywhere, every day, fear.

"Ma'am?" Private Scott appeared seemingly from out of nowhere.

She pressed a hand to her chest, aware that for once she'd not worn the black bombazine garment. The dress sorely needed cleansing. Earlier, she'd gone to the laundry and given it to one of the girls. The slave had taken it from her, giving her the oddest look, as though wanting to challenge her. But Angelina had shaken her head, warning her to not protest. She'd jerked her thumb over her shoulder at Sergeant Ross who seemed to trail her everywhere.

Angelina smoothed her work dress out around her as the handsome soldier approached, the osnaburg fabric practically screaming her status as former slave.

"Private, how can I help you?"

He clutched his gray hat in his large hands. The jacket as well as the pants were several inches short with the pants above his ankles and the jacket well above his sturdy wrists. Dark hair glistened on his arms sending a strange sensation through her. Unlike most men she'd encountered, she felt drawn to him with the sensation of ease, of comfort, waiting in his capable arms.

She could easily alter his clothing. It was a kindness she could perform.

"How does a gentleman get a bath around here? Ross wouldn't allow me to bathe with the others. I suspect he's angry that I got between him and you earlier today."

She shivered at the recollection of the Sergeant and what he might have done.

"Mrs. Carter, I don't know why you're staying out here." Private Scott ran a hand through thick dark hair, his hazel eyes inviting. Angie's pulse quickened.

Because I'm a freed woman and not a member of the family and these children are slaves. She opened her mouth but words failed to come.

"Mind if I sit with you for a spell?"

Charity grinned up at him but Julian eyed him suspiciously. Angelina scooted over and gestured for the children to do the same.

"No, we don't mind." His earlier comment was right, though—loathsome Ross likely was angry and Private Scott needed a bath. But the other field hospital odors made his masculine scent less powerful.

He held out his hand and passed a small carved soldier to Julian. No coloration, only that of the wood. No insignia to differentiate Union from Confederate. Just a soldier. A man.

As the boy examined the toy from all angles, his frown relaxed. "How'd you make this?"

"Whittled it—you want to learn how?"

"I want a lady—in a fancy dress." Charity pulled her skirt out at her side. Would this child ever have a chance to live a free life much less be a lady?

"Sure thing. First you have to have a block of wood to work with. I found these over at the ice house." Scott displayed a hunk of wood. It must have missed being ground into sawdust to keep the ice cold.

"Then you have to have a knife sharp enough to whittle with and a little flexible, like this one." He unsheathed a short knife.

Had another man done so she might have flinched but Angelina's only reaction was that of curiosity. Why did the Union army allow this man a knife? Had he stolen it?

Julian leaned in, placing an arm on the soldier's shoulder, as casually as he would have Abraham's in the field. The two of them, head-to-head looked so natural—so right. If only Julian could have a father. Charity placed a tentative hand on the man's other

47

broad shoulder and he beamed up at her, the cleft in his chin deepening.

Her heart swelled. He'd appointed himself her protector.

What would it be like to have a husband to look after her and defend her? To help with the children?

But she needed to go north. To start a new life.

"Children, scat to the laundry and ask Jemma to get a tub ready for Private Scott."

"It's Matthew Scott."

She chose to ignore his comment and averted her gaze. "You can bathe and then we'll get your uniform cleaned.

She'd put him into one of Hilly's uniforms or she'd fix what he had.

"Thank you ma'am."

Once the children departed, Matthew Scott stood, turned and glanced up at the façade of the Old House. He fixed his green-brown eyes on hers and his hand extended toward hers then stopped.

"Ma'am, you need to get yourself into that big house tonight. I can anticipate the next scene coming and it isn't a pretty one. I'm a theatrical manager, not a soldier, back home, and I know a villain when I see one."

She nibbled her lower lip. Mary B. told her they could sleep on the chaises in the hall landings on the third floor—they'd just need to bring quilts with them.

"Why do you think so?" What did he know?

"I heard Sergeant Ross boast that he was going to come visit you after he got cleaned up. He seems to think..." Angelina watched his wide mouth move, his lips move over perfect white teeth.

She leaned closer. What would it be like to have a man like this love her? Kiss her?

"Well, I don't know how to say this, but he doesn't believe you are a member of the family. And as such, he doesn't believe McClellan's protection extends to you."

Angelina stiffened. Did Mathew Scott also suspect? She pressed her fingers to her lips.

"And he seems to think that your placement in this building gives him access to you." Matthew's handsome face reddened. "I'm sorry."

Her mouth went completely dry.

Charity and Julian ran back to the porch. "Jemma say she ain't gonna do it—she tired."

Angelina glared at the child. "You know how to pump water and haul—you go back and do it for Mr. Scott."

"Thank you." His soft voice was barely audible. "I'm not a soldier, Mrs. Carter. I prefer Mister to Private as I am not an enlisted man."

Julian's pink tongue poked between his lips as though he might argue with his aunt, but then he ran off again, Charity chasing after him. How did they have any energy left after such a long day?

"Mrs. Carter?"

Distracted by her thoughts, Angelina looked around the room, as though Mary B. might have joined them but then she focused on Matthew Scott's eyes. So deep.

"Do you think you could get me a Union uniform, ma'am? Or perhaps a regular set of men's clothing—anything but this Confederate uniform."

The way he leaned toward her, the way his eyes darkened and lips parted reminded her of all the times she'd had to run from white men who'd caught her alone outside the house in one of the ancillary buildings. But unlike those men, she didn't fear him. Nor did his intent seem evil.

She drew in a long breath. "A Union uniform?"

He twisted his gray cap in his hands. "Surely you realize I've insisted from the beginning that I am a private citizen—conscripted against my will into the Confederacy."

"If that is so then why would you exchange one uniform for another?"

Chapter 4

After transferring their meager belongings yet again, Angelina found herself settled on the third floor landing of the Great House. As long as the Carter's slave cabins and almost as wide, the termination at the top of the stairs accommodated an assortment of chaise lounges and upholstered chairs. All were pressed back against the wall. Benches clustered near the windows for needlework, or by side tables with lamps and candles for reading. Here, Angelina and the children had placed their satchels. But they had no privacy. She'd worn Lorena's osnaburg servant's clothing—the black widow's gown still damp.

Angelina descended the curving stairway, the treads giving slightly with each step, a feature built into the design.

"Hold the rail, children." She needn't remind Charity, who gripped the walnut rail but Julian might skip down with nary a concern.

She shot a look at her nephew as he passed her on the left then disappeared from sight as he swiftly wound down and around.

Pants would make such a descent much easier. Still…the agile boy put her to shame.

At the bottom, though, Julian waited for her like a little gentleman. A smile twitched on his face and on her own. One day soon he'd be free. Educated. And earning a good living somewhere safe. Tears pricked her eyes.

Charity squeezed Angelina's hand and Julian took the other. They slipped into the parlor, wherein Mary B.'s raised eyebrows registered her disapproval. The surgeon and lieutenant, however, paid her no notice. Angelina exhaled slowly as she and the children settled on a settee below the open window, the cries of the injured carrying on the breeze. She cringed. They were about to have a late dinner at the house with the officers, then rest for the following day's work. But those men in the fields… What comfort would they receive? She sent up a silent prayer for them. And for herself and the children—she must get them north somehow. But the thought of traveling with the likes of Sergeant Ross made her stomach spasm.

Dr. Probst pointed to a cross-stitch sampler framed on the wall of the parlor. "Ladies, I presume you can sew?"

Louisa covered a giggle. Even Angelina knew the stitchery was from colonial days.

"Sir, do I appear so ancient?" Mary B.'s dry voice was accompanied by a slow smile, one dimple forming in her cheek. "Dr. Probst, I believe my husband's great-grandmother embroidered that sampler when she was a child."

Fanny set her teacup down. She glanced at Angelina. "My...cousin has a lovely hand at needlework."

How she wished Fanny hadn't diverted attention toward her. She pulled the children close in an attempt to hide Lorena's dress. She'd lost so much weight since leaving Mrs. Roat that her own clothing hung loose. And she'd not yet bothered to alter them, having paying jobs to finish first plus her chores for the Carters.

The man's red face began to lose its flush. He sniffed. "Good. I need someone to stitch the names of the deceased men into their coats."

Angelina squeezed the children's shoulders. She'd always sought to do God's will in her work. Whether constructing a fancy gown or repairing a ripped seam, she'd always prayed for the owner of the garment. But these severely injured men—they were going to the Lord. Going home. Her breath caught.

"I'm taking up a list of my dead but I don't know all the men's names. You'll have to ask the other injured if they know."

Mary B. nodded at Angelina. "Their mothers will be grateful—later."

What a horrid war. Shirley Plantation's mistress meant the mothers would rejoice when the bodies were finally brought home. And when would that be? A shiver coursed through her.

What of Private Scott's request to get him a union uniform? She'd prayed but God convicted her to not proceed. And even Hill Carter himself had come to her and cautioned her, "Don't do anything to rile these Yankees, Missy, do you understand?"

Mr. Carter rarely spoke to her. Why tonight?

"Come, gentleman, join me for a cigar before dinner." Hill Carter gestured to the hallway and the men rose and departed.

Turning toward Angelina, Mary B. angled her head. "Could you change into something less dreadful for dinner, Angie?"

Fanny sniffed. "We'd like to make ourselves presentable before dinner."

Angelina swallowed. Charity and Julian had never eaten at a fancy table. They'd have no idea what knives to use. "What about the children?"

The previous two nights she'd eaten with the children in the Old House, a cold supper of leftovers after a long day helping with the field hospital.

Louisa blinked at her. "The children will eat at a table in the parlor."

As soon as Louisa commented, Angelina realized her error. The Carter children had the custom of eating with their nurse in the parlor unless it was a holiday. When Angelina was a child, in the master's house in Charleston, she'd eaten in the kitchen house. But in Richmond, Angelina enjoyed the life of a companion to Mrs. Roat, and ate at the same lovely round oak table with her in her well-lit dining room.

As she grew older, Angelina spent her days in instruction under the French seamstress who trained her. All the while, Lorena toiled in the laundry at Shirley. Was it because Lorena's skin, a lovely light café au lait, was darker than her own—their fathers different? Mama never said what white man had fathered her, only that she'd born Lorena from love. What did it matter? Tears trickled down Angelina's cheeks. She'd been freed and placed with Mrs. Rose's older sister, a devout Christian. Although she'd allowed occasional visits to Shirley Plantation, Mrs. Roat didn't encourage the contact. And as far as Angelina knew, she never referred to

Angelina as anything other than "my ward and companion."

"Follow me." Louisa wagged a finger at Angelina. They trod the stairs up to the second story.

At the first landing a collection of overstuffed chairs, children's toys, games, and a cradle marked the floor as one where the Carter's grandchildren were kept with their mothers. How did the Carter babies sleep despite the groans of agony outside?

Louisa turned and continued down the long hallway. Bookcases, floor to ceiling, lined the long corridor leading to the bedrooms. She stopped before her bedroom's ornate door.

"Still can't believe my husband is gone from here." The two entered the spacious room.

Louisa crossed the wide floorboards to a huge chifferobe and opened one of its mahogany doors.

"Wear this." Louisa shoved a dark green gown at Angelina. "One of our aunts left it behind for repairs but I'd forgotten to give it to you."

The satin jacquard was exquisite.

Angelina fingered the fine material, recalling the days spent in the shop in Richmond—dreaming of opening her own establishment one day.

"There's a small tear on the side. Can you fix it before dinner?"

"Yes'm." Her face reddened as Louisa's cautioning eyes grew wide. "Thank you...Lou."

"You're welcome, Angie."

Angelina swiveled toward the window. "May I hold it up to the light?"

"Certainly." A crinkle formed in Louisa's brow. "Angie, Mama told me you refused to go north. Why?"

Skitters of nervousness wove up her arms as Angelina held the garment near the window. There was only a small flaw. Like there had been in Mrs. Carter's plan. Two small tears in the fabric of her life. Unlike the children, these rips could be repaired in under a quarter hour.

Lowering the dress, Angelina turned. "God convicted me to stay." To wait for Julian and Charity's freedom.

"Did Hilly have anything to do with that decision?"

Angelina's cheeks heated. "Perhaps. He prayed with me about it. As did Mary B. But I take responsibility for my decision." Poor though it was. While she'd considered taking the children in secret and going north with Diana and Paul Flowers, the Quaker couple advised her that such a trip was too risky at present. And prayers had again confirmed God's clear answer—*wait on Me.*

Nodding, apparently satisfied, Louisa bent by the bed, covered in a matelassé cover. She reached beneath and retrieved a small cigar box. "I think I have some thread to match."

She offered Angelina the box of needles, pins and threads.

Now, an hour later, attired in the expensive gown, her corset strings pulled too tight by Charity, Angelina wondered again at the wisdom of deceiving the northern officers into believing she was a member of the family.

But as long as Sergeant Ross believed so, she'd be content.

Matthew wasn't proud of his behavior, but he'd hidden in the widow's quarters at Angelina's request. Although he'd tried to convince himself it was to protect her, he'd also grown concerned as more and more wounded soldiers, union soldiers, had been loaded onto the boats departing up the James River. What was going on? He'd received a private message from Hill Carter, delivered by Angelina, to meet with him as soon as the sun rose the following morning.

Inside the Great House, he tapped lightly on Hill Carter's office door, just to the left as one entered the first floor.

"Come in." Mr. Carter's distinctive voice boomed through the office door.

Matthew entered and removed his hat.

"Have a seat, Mr. Scott—but first close the door."

Mister Scott. Not private Scott. Matthew's hands began to tremble.

"Do you enjoy the newspapers where you're from, Mr. Scott? In Ohio, I believe."

Matthew slid into the offered Windsor chair. "Yes, sir, I do."

The older man rubbed his chin, his green eyes sad. "Ever read the Richmond paper since you've been south?"

"No, sir." Where was he going with this conversation?

"Do you know I've had 17 children..." He paused as though recollecting something. "with my beautiful wife?"

No, sir." This sounded like the beginning of one of his father's lectures. Matthew had no siblings. No cousins. No aunts or uncles. He was alone in the world, save for his parents. But with Angelina, he'd begun to hope for a future. The beautiful Southern widow had given him hope. Dare he think it possible? Perhaps this was the topic on which the man wished to commence.

"We lost half our children." Moisture glistened in the man's eyes.

"I'm sorry sir. I pray one day, I too, will know the privilege of having a family."

"Pray you never experience the losses I have had."

"Yes sir, but I also hope to have a long marriage such as you've been blessed with." Why today had his tongue become unhinged? Because if he didn't say something to Angelina's uncle, he might never know if another marriage was in her future. And when? Was he already considering a Southern gentleman for her?

He fixed his eyes on Matthew as though looking through him and seeing someone else sitting there.

"My sons are all gone except Warrington. Thank God his services have been helpful here, to your northern comrades."

He believes me. He knows. Matthew rubbed the crick forming in his neck. "Dr. Carter has been most proficient."

"Mr. Scott, there is a notice in the Richmond paper." Hill Carter pulled a newspaper out from beneath a stack of ledgers.

He tapped at what appeared to be classified ads. "Your mother's name would be…"

Green eyes gazed at him, expectantly.

"Constance Merriweather Scott."

"Wife of Congressman Theodore Scott."

The dizziness, which had subsided, resumed and Matthew gripped the chair arms. "Yes."

Carter's surprisingly sympathetic eyes met his. "Your mother placed an ad in the Richmond Gazette. Perhaps hoping with the peninsula campaign finished that you or someone knowing of your location, might read this notice."

His heart squeezed. Carter pushed the paper toward him but Matthew's blurred vision made it hard to read. At least though, now it could be shown to the commanders of the Union troops, who'd been loading up wounded and shipping out upriver all day. He could go home. Or could he? The Union presence in southern Ohio had allowed the Confederates to take him, unimpeded.

"My children have both parents at home, awaiting their return." Hill Carter's voice grew sentimental.

Matthew nodded, which only made his head hurt more. He focused his eyes on the newsprint. *Constance Merriweather Scott, wife of Congressman Theodore Scott of Ohio, seeks whereabouts of son, Matthew T. Scott, conscripted into the Confederate...*

"I understand your father may not be able to return home until these hostilities have ceased."

Continuing to read, Matthew encountered the phrase "Grandfather has been notified." He re-read the paragraph. His grandfather, a wealthy New York banker, would exert whatever pressure he could to have Matthew returned.

"I attended the College of William and Mary with your grandfather, if he's Lafayette Merriweather."

Matthew swallowed. "Yes, sir, he is."

Hill Carter made a small sound in the back of his throat. "Copperhead newspaper owned by him up there."

Exactly—which was why Father had been swayed in that direction.

The door opened and Julian ran in. "Master, Confederate army is marching in— and Mr. Hilly is home!"

A cannonball seemed to have sunk into Matthew's gut.

"What?" Hill Carter rose. "My son is here?"

Julian ran back out.

Oh Lord, what now? And why had Julian called Mr. Carter Master?

The Carter women knew his declaration that he was not a Confederate soldier. And now Hill Carter had proof of his identity. What would he do with that information?

From the third floor window, Angelina spied a field of gray and butternut surging forward onto Shirley Plantation's fields.

"That's Mr. Hilly!" Julian loved the minister and had run down the stairs before Angelina could stop him.

A shiver went through her. God had provided. If she'd offered Matthew Scott the union uniform he'd requested then right now... He could be one of the Union wounded left behind, lying in Shirley's Fields. But even so, with the spells he still experienced, would he be taken to the Confederate hospital in Richmond? Had he listened to her advice and hidden himself in the Old House? Or had he gone?

Angelina descended the staircase, the thought of Matthew Scott's possible departure bringing her mood down, down, down as she marched, careful to avoid looking through the spiral center, which made her dizzy. Straightening her skirt she saw that Julian had left the door open to the office. With the Confederates now on the land, how should she address Mr. Carter?

She stood in the doorway and clasped her hands. "My instructions, sir?"

He waved a dismissive hand. "As before, Missy. Continue on. These are soldiers and you're…"

Mr. Scott rose and bowed toward her. Her heart lurched in her chest. He'd listened to her and was yet here. The open appreciation in his dark eyes caused her to flush. But the way he twisted his hat, she wondered what Mr. Carter had been discussing with him. Likely what he would do now that the Confederates arrived.

"Missy, take Mr. Scott, here, down to the Old House and get him settled in his room on the second floor."

Angelina glanced between Hill Carter and Matthew Scott. "Sir?"

"He can keep watch over you and the children there, also."

Sergeant Ross was surely gone.

She needed to make her way north, somehow, and get herself and the children to freedom. And with this influx of soldiers, her fortunes now seemed reversed. Still, she couldn't help the relief she felt over Matthew Scott remaining behind. What was she to do about her growing attachment to him?

"Missy, get him some of Hilly's old suits to wear."

"Sir?"

"Mister Scott is the son of one of my old college friends. He was conscripted into the army and is not a soldier. And with these spells he has, we don't want the soldiers getting any ideas that he might be going with them."

Her mouth hung open.

"Do you understand me, Missy?"

She licked her dry lips. "Yes sir."

But she didn't understand anything. And glancing at Mister Scott, he, too, appeared slightly perplexed.

Chapter 5

Matthew shuddered as Confederate soldiers marched forward up the Queen Anne forecourt toward them. Angelina leaned in toward him, a muscle in her cheek jumping.

The lieutenant strode toward the house, his sword slapping against his thigh. "Uncle Hill."

Several men trailed behind him. After rapidly ascending the porch steps, the officer briefly embraced Mr. Carter while the others remained at a respectful distance.

"Hard march for you, boy? You need a little fortification? A cigar?"

Carter's nephew grinned.

Matthew's heart hammered in his chest. Mr. Carter hadn't betrayed him. But he knew that in reality, Matthew was a private citizen, not a soldier.

"Come on up to the portico—bring your men, too."

"Need a bath and my trousers mended, Uncle. Can you get Angelina to help me?"

Why should she help him? The beautiful widow's posture stiffened beside him.

Hill Carter waved Matthew on. "The grandson of one of my old friends is visiting with us."

The officer's sandy eyebrows rose.

"He's staying in the Old House. You're welcome to quarters up on the third floor here, if you'd like."

Matthew broke out in a sweat. He shook hands with the men under the covered portico.

Hill Carter patted his arm firmly. "Shame Matthew here can't serve—he has spells, worse even than Hilly ever had. But he can help tend the wounded."

"Hilly's right behind me. Fit as a fiddle, too. Speaking of which—do you still have my old banjo here? I'd like to play later."

A dizzy episode commenced and Matthew had to grab the gray coated arm of Carter's nephew to avoid falling. Hill Carter's firm hand cupped his elbow. His vision cleared and Angelina's eyes, glittering in the sun, were wide, frightened—but for him or some other reason? Julian's words came back to him… Were she and the children slaves? His Abolitionist mother's daguerreotypes came to mind—of white children enslaved in Virginia.

"Angelina, would you accompany Matthew back? Best he lies down. I'm going to bring my nephew up to date on our doings here at Shirley."

She'd not been able to meet Matthew Scott's eyes when she'd gotten him to the Old House. Thankfully, he'd laid down for a rest. She'd used the opportunity to speak with Dr. Neill, who'd arrived with Mason Jeffries, a Carter nephew. The physician knew her only as Angelina Rose, seamstress from Richmond. He possessed the good sense to not inquire why she was at Shirley Plantation. She'd breathed a sigh of relief when he inquired about his sister's traveling gown. And was willing to pay as soon as she finished.

Angelina attempted to organize the pattern of her life again. If she could obtain one more gown order and receive payment, she'd have the full amount to pay off the Carters for her niece and nephew's freedom. With manumission papers in hand for all of them, could she travel North? Dare she risk it? She set about turning the parlor into her workroom and retrieved Miss Neill's ensemble, already partially constructed.

Angelina's hands shook as she carefully pressed pins into the jacket for Tara Neill, of Yorktown, who lived under Union occupation. Dr. Neill intended to have the outfit sent to Tara as a gift, sparing her the expense.

Thank God for Matthew, who had carried the dress form and her sewing machine over from above the laundry the previous evening. She ran her hands over the heavy brown fabric and frowned. Such dowdy fabric and color for such a lovely woman. Was Tara, like herself, trying to avoid notice? *Of course*— especially if she intended to travel, perhaps south to Florida where her wealthy sweetheart lived. Tara had obtained a special pass of protection to depart. If only she and the children possessed such a voucher.

"Aunt Angie, can I help?" Charity touched the brass crane pin cushion, screwed onto Angelina's worktable.

"Oh, yes…" Angelina had almost forgotten Charity, who rested atop a settee nearby.

Thankfully the Confederate army had sufficient help to tend to the union soldiers and she'd been given a reprieve. For now. But her chance for passage North had once again slipped through her fingers.

Tears dripped down onto the fabric remnants in her lap. "Come here, girl."

Charity wrapped a thin arm around Angelina.

"Stand back."

Her light eyes reflected hurt but she complied. Standing, Angelina held the fabric against Charity's back. She'd been performing their charade in several fussy dresses but Angelina hadn't the heart to put the child back into her house slave clothes which hadn't been replaced since the war began.

"How about you cut these pieces out to make you a new skirt?"

Her grin was quickly chased away by a wobbling frown. "What about Julian?"

Angelina waited for an explanation but none came.

"Aren't you gonna make him some clothes for our trip north?"

She couldn't reply—it was as though her tongue had been pinned to the roof of her mouth.

Her niece folded the pieces of cloth and moved close again. "When we leavin', Auntie Angie? Those men, they want to keep us slaves. I'm scared we never gonna get free."

Pulling the child into her embrace, the two wept together. And Angelina prayed.

A knock interrupted her entreaties to God.

The door to the house opened.

"Just me, Angelina—Hilly."

"And me!" Mary B.'s laughter carried to the back room.

Angelina sucked in a breath. Always before, Hilly's presence had the effect of bringing order to the household. His strong faith had a way of quieting nerves and inspiring hope. She chewed her lip. Had she allowed him to unduly influence her decision? Isaac and Phillip had scolded her before they swam to the gunboats, to freedom. *You shoulda gone, girl, instead of listenin' to that white man.* No, she couldn't blame anyone but herself. She didn't even blame God. Blaming accomplished nothing.

Charity ran to Hilly as he entered the room. She stopped when Mary B.'s eyebrows rose almost to her hairline. "Mr. Hilly, you home now?"

The stairs softly creaked, behind mother and son.

After taking several steps toward her, Hilly halted. "I owe you an apology, Angie. I didn't think war would break out."

He ran a hand back through his thick dark hair. "Everything happened so fast—Lorena's death, the contract we procured for you, and then this war breaking out and no one could accompany you."

Mary B. placed a hand on her son's arm. "What's done is done."

"Mama's right."

Angelina chewed her lower lip. "I was making so much money from orders, I thought I could more quickly pay off the debt." Never mind that the children were son and daughter of a local businessman who could have compensated the Carters. Part of her wondered why they should be compensated at all. Her ire rose at the thought that she, their free aunt, offered to care for them but Mr. Carter hadn't released them to her. Mrs. Roat thought it best that she go to Shirley and build a relationship with her niece and nephew before she hauled them off to Ohio. She appreciated the wisdom in that advice.

Mary B. shrugged then sighed. "Angie, if you don't mind, Cousin Mason has some mendin' he needs done. And I need Charity and Julian to help in the kitchen for all those hungry boys we've got to feed."

Hilly's apologetic smile did little to remove the sting of being reminded that she was a servant. These children, slaves.

Soft steps sounded on the carpet in the hallway and the Carters swiveled to look behind them.

"Lt. Carter?" Matthew Scott's voice carried. "You look well."

"What are you doing here, Scott? Why didn't you go with the Union army?"

Angelina caught his eyes, full of love, as he met hers. Guilt cinched her like a too-tight corset. She had to tell him soon.

Chapter 6

Six days tending the Confederate soldiers taxed Matthew. But he had the benefit of beginning and ending each day with Angelina and the children. Every minute he spent with them increased his desire to protect them. Her family clearly did not provide the emotional support she needed. Carter relations seemed to think they could simply drop their mending off with her night and day despite the fact that Angelina nursed soldiers in the field hospital and had children to tend to.

If they were invited up to the Big House for a meal, he might say something. He intended to discuss his irritation with Angelina that evening. Now, though, they must finish the task of burying the dead. How long would they lie there? What would their loved ones do? At least they could be identified now when they were disinterred.

Matthew finished burying the last of the Union deceased. Angelina had sewn all of the names into the jackets in a beautiful gold metallic thread that contrasted against the lining.

Hilly Carter prayed, his mother standing alongside him, a handkerchief covering her sweet face. A godly woman and her son.

The senior Hill Carter walked toward them, emerging from the Confederate encampment in his fields. He'd not revealed Matthew's identity to the army. Yet.

Mrs. Carter laid a gloved hand over her son's arm, and he tucked her grasp inside its crook.

"Thank God McClellan gave you a pass and protection, Mama—you may have need of it soon."

The plantation owner joined them and kissed his wife's cheek.

Mrs. Carter cast a meaningful glance at her son. "Do you have word?"

"Some intelligence."

Face sagging in defeat, Hill Carter wiped at his brow. "I want to meet you up at the house, son, but first I wish to speak with Mister Scott."

Matthew felt his cheeks blanch, despite the hot humid day. Even the birds had ceased singing as the sun rose higher.

Hilly Carter compressed his lips but then nodded in Matthew's direction. "May God bless you as you seek His will for you, Mister Scott."

"Thank you." He wished the same for the officer, but couldn't manage the words.

Mother and son strolled off toward a small carriage, its twin bay horses tethered nearby.

Green eyes roamed Matthew's face. "Bet you wonder why they haven't taken you back to Richmond."

"Yes, sir, I have." He removed his cap and shoved his hand through his slick hair. He sorely needed another bath. The James River washes weren't sufficient. Perhaps that night he'd once again bathe in the laundry and use the fragrant bayberry soap Angelina had given him.

"I was a naval officer. You are a noncombatant."

No. He had been a combatant. Fired on his own countrymen. Bile rose up in his throat.

"We've word that the Union armies will soon arrive. Your opportunity to return home is nigh—that is if the officers in charge don't take strong exception to your father and his political leanings."

Matthew cocked his head. "Sir, I greatly fear they shall."

The plantation owner nodded. "I've something else to share with you since you've become so fond of our Angelina."

The older man glanced around and Matthew followed his gaze. There was no one within a stone's throw of them.

"Angie refused a chance to go North when my wife gave her the opportunity." His mouth tightened. "In fact, she was to have assisted with your theatrical troupe—with the stitching and so forth. I came across my records of the agreement only yesterday. My wife and I kept our word, we would have sent her, but she declined."

"With Scott's Theatrical Troupe?" Now likely defunct.

"She's a freed woman and can make her own choices."

Freed woman? "You mean…"

Those intent eyes fixed on Matthew's again. "Angelina was a freed woman, living in Richmond, training to be a seamstress. Mighty fine one, too."

Matthew stretched his neck, suddenly stiff.

Mr. Carter surveyed him with a slow deliberateness that caused Matthew to feel as though he'd just been judged. "Her owners in South Carolina gave manumission papers to Angie but not to Lorena. Mary and I purchased her sister, a good worker although she was too easily swayed by one of our local boys…" He rubbed his chin.

Matthew swallowed. His Angelina had been a slave. "The children?"

Mr. Carter gave him a look of warning.

By rights they were his slaves. A sick feeling formed in Matthew's gut. *I have my own little acting troupe here at Shirley Plantation*—one with a female lead acting the part of a Southern Belle and two slave children the part of her doting children. No wonder she hadn't left. She must have needed to free the children.

"It's true." Angelina's knuckles turned white as she gripped the shield back of a cherrywood chair in the Flanker's dining room.

No wonder they'd had Angelina, the children, and him eat in the Old House while under Confederate occupation.

His mother, if she yet lived—how would she receive a daughter-in-law who had been a slave? A woman of color. Yet Mother was a staunch Abolitionist. Would she stand by her convictions and accept a freed woman as his wife? And what about the children?

"Feel free to reject me." Despite her scowl, Angelina's face remained beautiful. Perfect—as God had intended it to be.

He twisted his handkerchief together. She'd accepted a contract with his company yet hadn't fulfilled it. Could she not keep her word? "Why didn't you come to Ohio and work for me?"

"What?" Her lush lips fell open revealing her even teeth.

"You were supposed to get on a train and arrive before my season began in 1861. What prevented you?"

"I..the children of course." Her brow wrinkled. "I couldn't leave them."

Or was it something else? Like her affection for the Carter family and for Hilly Carter in particular. A married man. While Matthew shared her faith, he had great difficulty in understanding why she hadn't come to Ohio and sent for the children later. But who was he to judge? He'd never been in her shoes, thank God.

Chapter 7

The first week of July had passed when new Union soldiers swept in with a determined efficiency. While Matthew should be relieved at the Confederates' departure, he wasn't sure the Union army would give him any assistance in returning home.

Dr. Warrington Carter, who'd called him to the Great House, rose from the office settee, his medical satchel in hand. "Mister Scott, I believe Papa wants you to write your Mama—believes we'll be able to get mail North now. And while I greatly value your assistance with the wounded men, I'm not so sure Lieutenant Maher will."

"I see."

"Might be best for you to help elsewhere—I'm sure Papa can find work for you."

"Yes, sir."

After waving a slim hand toward his father's desk, Dr. Carter departed, almost silently, from the room. A gentleman's gentleman, he seemed too genteel for what he was going out into. Matthew had almost adjusted to the continual moaning that emanated from the fields and carried on the humid winds.

Now to ask his mother to petition the President. Had she already—for Father and himself?

Matthew slid into the seat behind Mr. Carter's mahogany desk. After gathering his writing implements he commenced. After he finished his letter, he dusted the missive with sand and allowed it to dry, chuckling at the thought of sealing it with an ornate brass crest from the Hill family from the late 17th century. Almost two hundred years old. This family had deep roots to the land and community. What of his past? Father's silence on the subject deterred him from digging deeper.

Glancing outside, his heart leapt as he caught sight of gold and bronze ringlets glowing in the sun as Angelina, head bent, lifted her skirts and jounced up the steps of the house.

The heavy hall door opened and Matthew rose from the desk, his cheeks heating with anticipation of seeing her. And with the notion that somehow they could now put their differences aside and make plans to return to his troupe in Ohio. From there they could travel to the field hospitals and entertain the soldiers. He'd not let war kill his dreams.

The door swung in. "Matthew. Mr. Scott..." Angelina's flushed face and quick breaths alarmed him.

He closed the distance between them and grasped her shoulders. "What is it?"

She looked up at him, her blue-gray eyes wet. "Granny is dying."

"I'm so sorry. But I thought you had no family here, other than the children." He handed her his handkerchief and she wiped her nose.

"You don't understand."

A hazy recollection of the strange woman who'd spoken with him at the field hospital, when he'd been so ill, returned to him now.

Angelina boldly grasped his hand and pulled him into the hall. Mrs. Carter, her arms full of bedsheets earmarked for bandages, blinked at them.

"It's Granny," Angelina called over her shoulder. As though that should explain.

"I'll join you shortly."

They strode on through field after field of tents, soldiers, medical personnel, and the stench of death. Yet Matthew's heart ascended. The freed woman declared her affections for him by walking hand in hand with him through the plantation—the men's jealous glances affirming so. Matthew glanced down at her, admiring the way her lips set in determination and her chin jutted ever so slightly.

"Can you tell me about Granny?"

Glittering eyes flashed at him as though he ought to know, but he didn't. An ache formed at his temple. "I need to take it a little slower, please."

She halted and released his hand. "I'm sorry, I forgot—you've been doing so well."

"Yes, I have." He wiped his brow with the sleeve of Hilly Carter's summer suit, a crisp tan linen given to him by the man before the southern troops had hastily departed ahead of the Union's return to Shirley Plantation.

"Ready?" The way her lips puckered, lured him closer. "I'll keep your pace, Matthew."

"I prefer Matt. After all, I shall convince you to marry me." He offered her what he hoped was a charming grin.

"Matt, then." She smiled, her lips only a breath away. So close, if he leaned down, he could kiss her right there, right at the edge of the Union encampment.

Several soldiers walked past and laughed as they took in Matthew and Angelina.

The "Widow Carter" appeared much more attractive in dusky rose than in black. And with the alterations she'd managed on Louisa Carter's hand-me-downs, the effect was startling.

"Come on." He tucked her arm in his and they strode on as though all the world might know she was his and he was her beloved. But he'd not yet shared the words with her. Till now.

He swallowed. They passed the end of the row upon row of tents, Angelina's gaze fixed on the far-off slave cabins.

"Angelina, I love you."

"What?" She paused.

"I said I love you. And I want to marry you."

Thick dark lashes beat like hummingbird's wings. "Even though…"

"Sh…" he pressed a finger to her lips, warm beneath his touch. "It doesn't matter. All I care about is whether you'll come with me. Marry me." He'd have knelt right there in the mucky field were he not in Lt. Carter's suit.

Angelina rolled her lips together and began to cry. She took his hand and again tugged him onward. Was that her answer? Was she refusing him?

"I…I had wanted to take you to Granny because…" She stifled a sob.

"You said she's dying. I'm sorry."

Tears freely streamed down her cheeks. She wiped them with her hands.

His head throbbed. "Why did you want me to come?" With the increased pain in his head came the memory of a grizzled elderly woman bent over him in the field and Angelina beside her.

"Do you remember when you first arrived?" She wiped her nose with his handkerchief.

"What did Granny mean about me looking like someone?" A chill of recognition crept up his spine as he recalled her words—and that she knew the names of his grandparents.

"Matt, what did your parents tell you about your family?"

"Only that my father's family was from Virginia and that we had no family members on his side—that my paternal grandparents were dead." He rubbed his chin. The letter he'd seen contradicted his father's assertion.

"Do you know what Granny said about you?" Angelina lifted her skirts as they approached the quarters.

He shrugged.

"She said now she could die."

"Why?" Chills ran up his back.

"Granny said now her vision had come true."

Matthew sighed. Superstitious nonsense, but he'd humor Angelina.

Angelina led him to the first cabin, surprisingly large, perhaps about 20 feet long—bigger than many of the log cabins around home in Ohio. They entered the well-swept structure, meeting not the odor of death but the scent of bacon grease, cold ashes, and dried fruit and tobacco.

"There he be." Granny pointed a bony arm in his direction.

A stout woman, the color of strong coffee, raised the frail woman's head from her shabby pillow. The caregiver narrowed her eyes at Matthew, her expression angry.

"Sit there."

Angelina continued to cry. She sat next to Granny, taking the place of the other woman, who left the cabin muttering something beneath her breath. Unease gripped Matthew.

"I see you now, boy, and you be well—now I can go on to heaven." Her lips flattened into a satisfied smile.

Patting the woman's wrinkled hand, Angelina bent and kissed her brow. "Granny Scott, don't say that…"

Matthew's head jerked up. He licked his lips and moved closer to the rustic bed, made from what appeared to be four narrow tree trunks.

"It be true—my dreams come true." Her voice resonated beautifully. How marvelous she'd sound in a theater.

"God told me in a vision—your descendant gonna come back to you in a soldier's uniform."

A chill went down Mathew's arms. Was he a descendant of this slave woman? This poor dying soul? He took one of her hands, dry as a corncob, recollecting her words as he'd lain in the field. "You said you had a son and daughter—Theodosius and Eulalie…Scott?"

She closed and then opened her rheumy eyes as though agreeing. "Eulalie a fine girl and Master Scott's son love her—he do. They go to Kentucky long time ago. Her father white." Granny Scott gave a sharp nod as though Matt should know this.

He swallowed.

Angelina dipped a cloth into a basin of water nearby but when she made to press it to Granny's forehead the woman swatted her hand away. "I be 92 years now. I be goin' home soon but I ain't sick, child."

Above the fireplace, on a narrow mantel, a pencil sketch of a prosperous-looking man and woman was set inside an inexpensive picture frame. Granny followed his gaze.

"Go look. That be my baby girl and her husband."

When she released her hand from his and then waved it birdlike at him, Matthew stood and went to look. The man's face resembled his own. High cheekbones were shaded. His lips were the same shape and he even had the slight mocking uplift to his right corner. His shoulders were broad, like his own, and his arm rested protectively around the shoulder of the woman beside him—a woman whose features were more African than European, and whose hair was shown as waving gently around her narrow shoulders. There was something endearing about the way she was portrayed.

"That be done when they young—like you. They have a son and a passel of daughters."

"The son's name?"

The elderly woman stared at him. "You know, boy."

Embarrassment caused him to feel all of five-years-old—standing in the kitchen, his Father yelling at him to never inquire again about his ancestors.

"In those visions God sent me, you always wearin' a gray uniform. I never understand. Then when the South choose them colors I prayin'—Lord have mercy, don't tell me my great-grandson gonna show up here with a band of Confederate soldiers."

Tears flowed down Angelina's cheeks and two tiny drops coursed down Granny's.

"Yet there you be lyin' on the ground and I be wonderin'—did Theodosius's and

Eulalie's son despise his past so much he done workin' to keep his own people in slavery?"

"My father never said…"

Angelina kissed the top of the elderly woman's head. "I'm sure he thought he was doing what was best for his child—passing as white and starting a new life for himself."

Patting her hand, Granny looked up. "You do the same, girl, and don't you regret it. Don't you look back. My great-grand, he gonna get you and those children up north—you'll see."

Her great-grandson. The past he knew nothing about had caught up with him. Matthew struggled to wrap his mind around what the slave woman was saying. His own great-grandmother—enslaved here. "What can I do for you, Granny?"

"Nothin'—you already done it. I can go home to Jesus now that you be here and now the Union soldiers stayin'.

Moisture pooled in his eyes. This altered script for his life left him as confused as though someone had changed all his lines to Greek. Yet everything, his whole life, Father's strange behavior all made sense. He was the descendant of a slave woman. He'd returned to Shirley Plantation from whence his grandparents had left decades earlier to begin a free life together. God had brought him full circle. His father had chosen to leave his family behind—to deny them. At a cost. Perhaps not to Theodore Scott, but to his son.

Matthew had no family other than his mother's wealthy parents in New York. And his Abolitionist-minded mother had rebelled and fled from them, in marriage to a political upstart from Ohio. What would his Copperhead grandfather think? And would he help Matthew if he knew?

Chapter 8

September 1862

How he'd consented to almost three long months toiling in the fields of Shirley Plantation, Matthew couldn't figure. One day had seemed to blend into the next and one need turning into hundreds of others. Without food they'd not be able to feed the family nor the troops. With his dizzy spells subsiding, he'd gained strength by toiling alongside the field workers. Some days it was as though he was doing penance for something, perhaps his father's turning his back on his people. Other times, he allowed himself to experience the labor as though he was a slave.

A bent figure, leaning heavily on a gnarled wood cane, awaited him at the edge of the field. Granny Scott lifted her grizzled head as he approached.

"Matthew, boy, come sit a spell."

"Yes, ma'am." He wiped his brow.

His great-grandmother's smile spread like honey on hot cornbread she now offered him.

"Thank you, Granny." He tried to imagine his wealthy grandmother

Merriweather meeting Granny Scott and stifled a chuckle.

"You bring your banjo down to the cabin tonight, boy?"

"Yes, ma'am." He laid his suntanned hand over her ashy ebony fingers and squeezed gently. "I'll bring Angie and the kids, too." Sounded like they belonged to him.

"It comin', boy, you know." She rocked gently on her cane. "Like the good book promise in eternity but I gonna get it sooner, I think."

"Granny?"

"Freedom. I gots dreams every night now. Freedom comin'. For me and all us colored folks. Freedom for you, too, Matthew. You can be whoever you want to be and not who your Mama or Daddy make you be."

How much of his acting had been in reaction to his father? To his mother? He'd found, in helping Hill Carter, that he enjoyed farming. Not that he'd relish being enslaved here. But it had suited his nature better than hospital work did. And Dr. Probst as well as Dr. Carter believed that good nourishment was essential to the soldiers' recoveries.

"I pray you are right, Granny." Matthew scratched the stubble on his face.

Mother's recent letter told of Father's sojourn to Canada. After her protest to the president, Father had been released—to the Confederate army. She'd been furious and Grandfather was intervening and had traveled to Washington.

"Here—your family now."

Trodding across the fields, Angelina approached, a child in each hand. A smile split her beautiful face. She released Charity and Julian and they ran, waving their hands wildly.

The desire to embrace her in his arms consumed him.

"This be it." Tears rolled down Granny's precious face.

"He freed us, Granny, he freed us!"

Carter or Lincoln? Regardless if Hill Carter freed the children, where would they go? Matthew wasn't safe anywhere. Not as the son of Congressman Theodore Scott.

"President Lincoln emansupperation us!" Charity threw herself into Matthew's arms and he lifted her into the air. She smelled of sunshine, earth, and sweet tea.

"E-man-sup-ated." Julian sounded out the word.

As he set the little girl down, Angelina came to his side and whispered in his ear. "Lincoln hasn't made it official yet—"

Granny prodded him with her cane. "You go on and give her a hug. She special. She be mother of my great-great-grands one day."

She laughed softly as Matthew pulled Angelina into his arms, her soft embrace balm for his soul yet exhilarating, too. Mother of his children—he liked the sound of that.

"Come on, I'm going to play this banjo. I've got a song for you." Matthew grinned at them, wondering what they'd think of the words. He'd written about waiting, longing, and ultimately—leaving together. He'd come to his great-grandmother's and grandmother's home, if it could be called such. But he'd kneeled last night and asked God to take him, Angelina, and the children to freedom.

But where could they be free from the armies and from bounty hunters who might snatch any of them and sell them in the deep south? They could do the same to him, yet he'd never had to consider it before. One drop of blood. Someone who thought that way could easily rationalize selling Matthew into slavery as a black man. What was he? *A child of God.*

November of 1862 came swiftly. For the first time in Matthew's life he had to ensure the fruits of harvest would be ready to produce some semblance of a Thanksgiving meal. The officers at nearby Berkeley Plantation asked for them to honor the day. Berkeley claimed to have hosted the first

Thanksgiving. God was still on His throne. And Angelina seemed to be falling in love with him, too.

They stood in the parlor of the Old House, arms wrapped around one another, foreheads pressed together. The children helped in the kitchen with the noon meal. Soup—generously laced with greens thanks to the crop yield, cornbread with butter, and weak tea sweetened with molasses awaited the men. For dinner there would be a hearty pumpkin stew with venison. His stomach growled.

"If we weren't living in the same house, I might let you kiss me." Angelina's tone teased but he sensed the underlying seriousness of her comment.

"I might just steal me a kiss, anyway." Matthew leaned in, Angelina's blue-gray eyes widening, her lips parting slightly.

He inhaled her verbena soap and nuzzled her neck. When she sighed, he grinned and pulled away. Best control himself.

The door flew open and the flames in the fireplace danced.

"Mr. Carter got a letter for you, Uncle Matt." Julian hollered down the hallway.

"Come here, Julian." Angelina's lips compressed as she backed away from him.

"What?" His petulant tone reminded Matthew of his own when he was a child.

"Who is it from?"

"He don't tell me, just say Uncle Matt should come. Now." The boy turned and ran back out of the house.

Angelina and Matthew both sighed. Then laughed.

After pulling on his wool overcoat, one of Hilly's from his days at seminary, Matthew headed over to the house.

When Matthew entered the office, Carter waved an envelope at him.

"Your Father sends word."

Father. "Thank you."

"Have a seat."

Scanning the missive, Matthew drew in a deep breath of relief and held it, then slowly exhaled. "My father is in Windsor, Canada—across the river from Detroit." But how to get to him?

"If it were within my power to loan you the money to get you there, I would. You've worked harder than any overseer I've ever had on this plantation."

"Thank you, sir." Did any of the slaves ever receive thanks for their hard work? A vein throbbed in Matthew's temple. Still, he'd been glad to help salvage what they could of the crops so that the army and the family could be fed. They'd had some of the recovering soldiers take short stints in the fields when the late crops came in. How grateful they'd all been for greens and vegetables that still grew in the southern climates in late fall. And they could celebrate, albeit modestly, with the Berkeley owners, relatives of the Carters.

"Mr. Scott, I will understand if you are ready to leave. But your Grandfather—well, he won't receive my letter about my lack of immediate funds for a spell. I feel sure he'll get money to you once he receives my mail. I am sorry to cause you delay."

Horses' hooves clattered up the carriageway then continued on, as though the riders galloped onto the Queen Anne forecourt. The sounds of someone wailing outside carried through the window.

Hill Carter crossed to the window. "Two Confederate soldiers."

Matthew joined him. "Isn't that your son Hilly's horse?"

Several Union cavalrymen trotted up but stopped behind the other two. A man lay horizontal across the back of the black gelding.

Mr. Carter pressed a hand to his chest. "My sons…"

Angelina watched, numb, as Hilly Carter's casket was lowered into the ground in the family cemetery. Nearby his widow sobbed into her father-in-law's shoulder while

Mary B.'s glassy eyes remained unfocused, staring past them all.

He never should have gone. Of all the boys, Hilly belonged at home. A man of the cloth, someone whose seizures had affected his life – why had he enlisted? Now his poor mother and widow and family were left to grieve him. *I am left to grieve. Oh, Hilly, how could you?*

Matthew's arm wrapped around her shoulders and drew her closer. They stood in the back of the group, at a distance, but Angelina could hear every word the pastor said. Why, why, why? He'd broken his mother's heart. She'd never be the same again. And something in Angelina twisted, too. Hilly had been a man of God. But he'd not been spared. And he'd been wrong in his thinking. In error about fighting for a nation that would keep many of its citizens enslaved. But he'd been a Christian man. How could he justify his actions? He, like all of them, would stand before God and give an account of his life.

She shivered. What about her? Would her account to the Lord be lacking? Matthew's grandfather had yet to send money. *Lord, what would you have me do? Tell me Lord.*

1863

"President Lincoln's emancipation proclamation has become law." Angelina fed Granny Scott thin broth as she sat up in bed.

Granny sipped slowly, her strength in recent weeks fading. "You free now, Angie girl—you and Matthew take those sweet children and go."

"We're free, Aunt Angie." Charity grinned up at her from the rocker, where she knit a scarf for her brother who'd just returned from fetching more wood for the chilly cabin.

Butler's troops lay positioned across the river from Shirley. He seemed to be spying on them. And he'd construed Hilly's death and burial as some kind of ploy to deliver Confederate news via the Carter family. When boats appeared at the boat landing and emancipated slaves—now soldiers—appeared, she couldn't believe her eyes. And when they were placed as sentries at Shirley's gates, Hill Carter had a fit. He sent a protest believing Butler deliberately slighted the family. The general relented and then sent white soldiers as sentries. But the appearance of the black soldiers had inspired a thrill of hope and pride rippling through the slaves in the cabins.

Angelina held another spoonful to Granny's trembling lips. "Mr. Carter is still being held by the army." As was Dr. Carter, who was sorely needed at the hospital, with so many men still struggling to recover.

Granny's filmy eyes showed no surprise. "You and Matthew and the children—you go tell that General Butler to let old Master Carter come home. And you tell him to send you North. As far as that man will send you."

Was God speaking to her through Granny? The Lord had been telling her something similar even before the army had come and taken Hill Carter and Dr. Carter across the river. That had been several days ago. She shivered. Would they hurt them?

A quick rap on the cabin door preceded Mary B.'s entrance into the cabin. She closed the door behind herself as Julian placed another log in the fireplace.

Mrs. Carter, whose demeanor had utterly changed since her son's death, stared up glassy-eyed at Angelina. "Warrington had brought down the chests from the attic— winter clothes. He did that before those foul men came and dragged him and his father off. I want you to go through them and gather up bundles for your trip to Ohio. God is surely telling me you shall need them. And that you will receive favor. Go to that beast, Butler, and tell him the truth about my husband. Oh Angelina…"

The matron collapsed in sobs into Angelina's arms. She patted Mary B's back, the scent of rose water a comfort that somewhere, inside this shadow, was the godly woman she knew.

Stepping away, Mary B. wiped at her tears with an embroidered handkerchief, Hilly's. "I can't bear to lose them. What if…"

"You won't. They can't." But would they?

They called Butler a beast but the slaves looked to him like a Messiah—and the ticket to the Promised Land. Might he help her? Would God use a gruff man like the general to bring about His will?

Matthew stepped from the boat and assisted Angelina and the children down onto the pier. "We're here to see General Butler."

They were ushered into his presence, the soldier's faces grim. They'd been at the dock, sending Hill and Warrington Carter back across the river. Both men shaky but unharmed.

Matthew stood, his hat clutched in his hand. "I'm grateful you released Mr. Carter and his son."

General "Beast" Butler glanced up from his campaign desk. "How might I assist?"

Matthew pulled himself up to his full six feet. "General Butler, sir, I am the son of congressman Scott of Ohio. I was conscripted in the Confederate Army seven months ago."

The general ceased shuffling his pile of papers. "Heard about that."

"I'd like to respectfully request that you aid us in traveling to Ohio."

"I know your father." Butler glared at Matthew.

He swallowed, sensing his freedom ebbing away with the James River.

Butler sneered at him. "Hear he's hiding in Canada now."

Getting Angelina and the children there might be a better option than Ohio, but with Butler's caustic tone, he might end up in the stockade.

His legs trembled and he did what actors did to reduce the annoying tremors and slacked his hip, bending his other leg, attempting to fool his body into an air of nonchalance.

"Your father's own supporters don't know what to do about him."

Angelina squeezed his arm. Butler still hadn't asked them to sit.

The union commander stood. "Makes me wonder why you'd think you could bring a Southern belle and her two rebel whelps in here and ask me to send them north with you."

"Sir, if I may?" Angie took two steps forward. "I'm a free woman, a former slave."

The general's eyebrows rose. "And the children?"

"My sister's children—slaves, now freed by President Lincoln." Pride shone in her strong features.

The man grinned. "Yes, ma'am, you are standing on United States occupied soil."

She clutched her reticule, inside which were funds she'd received from her gowns—not needed to free the children. "We only ask that you allow us to travel with your wounded, north, to freedom."

He rubbed his chin. "Long haul for you."

"I can help tend to the injured and the children can give them water and run errands."

"And you, Mister Scott—do you wish us to carry you to the closest railroad? You could wire your mother for funds."

Angelina patted her purse. "I've enough, I believe, to get us there."

"Do you indeed, Miss..."

"Soon to be Mrs. Matthew Scott." Angelina swiveled toward him.

She'd never said that she loved him, but she didn't have to—the look on Angelina's glowing face said it all.

General Butler's eyebrows raised, then lowered. "I see. Perhaps Mrs. Scott's abolitionist viewpoints carried some weight then."

God had put them together. In His perfect time.

Julian and Charity grasped his hands.

Butler held out a broad hand. "Wait a minute, I've got someone I want to send with you."

Angelina's long black eyelashes fluttered against her creamy skin. Soon she would be his wife. And these children his own.

The General stood. "Private Carlton, call that trumpet player down here, would you?"

The previous summer, the forlorn strains from a bugler had echoed across from Harrison's Landing. Matthew missed the small orchestra who accompanied his theater troupe.

"Sir?" the fresh-faced Private Carlton reddened, his eyebrows raised.

"The one from Ohio who swam out to the gunboats from the Wyatt plantation last summer."

"Yessir." Carlton saluted, then turned sharply and exited the room.

Julian pulled free and approached the desk.

"Julian, no!" Angelina exhaled loudly.

Butler shrugged and motioned the boy forward. "You want to ask me something, son?"

"Where's Ohio?"

Tears pricked Angelina's eyes. Ohio was the place she should have gone to long ago. Where she could have sent for the children. Where they could have been spared these long horrid months of war. Where... A black man entered the room, hat in hand.

"You called for me, sir?" The man's dark eyes darted to her and the children.

"Yes." Butler stroked his jaw. "You said you wish to return home instead of serving your country."

Angelina felt pity for the man, who now stared at his feet, clad in too-big shoes, army-issue.

Matthew squeezed her hand. "Excuse me, General Butler, but I think I know this man. Frank, is that you?"

The stooped man straightened and his eyes caught Matthews. "Mr. Scott?" A grin split his face.

"What are you doing here?" A gleam lit Matthew's eyes and Angelina glanced between the two men.

"Could ask you the same." Frank closed the distance between himself and Matthew and the two men shook hands.

Butler chuckled. "Well, then, I guess it shall be no chore for Frank to accompany you home."

Julian peered up at the General. "Does that mean Aunt Angie has to pay for him?"

Rubbing his chin, the man nodded. "Afraid so, little man."

"Humph!" Julian crossed his arms, looking so much like an imitation of the General that she had to laugh.

Charity touched Frank's arm. "Can you tell us about Ohio?"

"Were you a slave there, mister?" Julian's lower lip worked in a pout.

"No, I was not—my family was always free—from the time we arrived in what is now New York, but back then it was called New Netherlands. That was a long time ago, though."

"Then, why…"

Angelina cut Julian off despite her own interest. "That's enough now, we'll have our whole trip for you to pepper him with questions."

Frank smiled. "Yes, ma'am, you got that right. It's a long haul up there."

Butler settled back into his chair. "Mrs. Carter or Mrs. Scott, or whatever her name is…"

"Miss Rose," she supplied.

Matthew squeezed her hand. "Until we find a church or a courthouse where we can marry."

Angelina pressed her hand into her pocket and felt the circle of gold, safely stitched into its own tiny fabric square inside. Mrs. Roat had gifted her with a wedding ring that could no longer slide over her arthritic fingers. Matthew would have something to place on her finger—

Soon.

The General cleared his throat. "In any event, Miss Rose here will cover your expenses on your trip to Ohio, Frank."

His large eyes met hers and he smiled. "Thank you, Ma'am."

Matthew laughed. "He'll pay you back once he's back to work with the theater."

"You have a black man in your orchestra?" Her niece's light eyes widened as she stared up at Matthew, her soon-to-be husband.

"Not exactly an orchestra—more like a small band. And yes, my mother insisted. My mother, the Abolitionist, married to a man she hoped would take her far from her father's harsh ways. Instead she'd ended up with a Copperhead congressman trying to pass for white who kowtowed to her father." His Adam's apple bobbed as he swallowed. "And I pray I still have a theatrical company when I return."

She hoped so, too. Elsewise, how would they live? God would provide. "If you don't, you'll at least have a seamstress."

Matthew bent and brushed his warm lips gently against her cheek. She blushed and pressed a hand to her face.

Frank laughed. "And a trumpeter."

"We can act, can't we, Julian?" Charity's chin shot up.

A sergeant entered the room. "We have transport ready, sir."

Charity held her arms up and although Angelina shook her head at the child, she too, hadn't expected so much walking. But the soldiers who accompanied them to the train station didn't have extra mounts nor much wagon space for her and the children, much less the men. So they'd walked some, together.

"We'll be to the station, soon." One that could connect to railroad lines still operational or to where they could obtain alternate transportation.

Her niece turned to Matthew. "Can you carry me, Uncle Matt?"

"He ain't our uncle." Julian pouted.

Oh no, was rebellion already rearing its head in the child? Angelina cringed.

But the boy peered up at Matthew with adoration. "He's gonna be our Pa, aren't you?"

Charity looked down from where she now perched on Matthew's shoulder. "Sure he is, aren't you?" She patted his cheek.

Matthew brushed a kiss against the child's forehead and she giggled.

Frank laughed. "I can hardly wait to wrap my arms around my children again."

What had happened to the man? "How did you end up in Virginia, Mr. Mullen?"

He blew slowly out of his mouth and she could imagine him warming up to play his trumpet. She'd make him a fine broadcloth suit and tailor it to fit him—not like the ill-fitting clothing he now wore.

"Oh, I was just minding my own business, Miss Rose. Was practicing for the music for Our American Cousin, Miss Keene's show. I was called outside by Mr. Booth, the new fellow, and the next thing I knew someone hit me over the back of my head." Frank rubbed absently at the back of his short kinky hair.

Julian's eyes grew wide. "Who hit you?"

Matthew's eyes narrowed. "Booth went out ahead of me right before I left."

"He wasn't there when I woke up—just two men who claimed to be bounty hunters and said I belonged to some man in Virginia.

Didn't care that I was a freed man. Laughed. Said they'd be paid regardless."

"All the way into south Ohio?" Angelina's voice came out a croak.

"Yes, ma'am, that was almost three long years ago, now."

You waited. "Frank, we did our last performance that night—July 1860." Matthew squeezed her hand so hard that she pulled free.

Ahead, she caught sight of the station.

You obeyed.

Angelina ran her hands up and down her arms to quell the prickles that danced over them. "I was contracted to sew the clothing for the production."

Frank paused, as did Matthew and the children.

Up ahead, the grating of metal against metal announced a train slowing.

"Ma'am?" Frank perused her face hard. "You look every bit a white lady but if you had been there and those criminals got wind that you were in fact a freed woman…"

The words hung in the air. They would have taken her with them. Who knows what they would have done. She shuddered, unable to control the tremors coursing through her body.

Matthew lowered Charity to the ground and pulled Angelina into his strong embrace.

She leaned into his chest, burying her face and inhaling the soothing scent of bayberry soap and his own masculine scent. He pulled away, his hazel eyes darkening as he leaned in to kiss her. She didn't hesitate, but tipped her head back to accept his firm warm lips on her own, her heart hammering in her ears above the din of the station. Satisfaction flowed through her. He deepened the kiss and pulled her so close to him that she felt his ribcage expand when he released her, sighing. This would be her husband, her protector. But God had kept her safe, too—by warning her. By putting people around her to caution her. By speaking to her through His Word.

You are truly free.

She didn't care how loud, smoky, smelly, or crowded her first train ride would be. It would be right on schedule—at God's appointed time.

THE END

Editorial Notes

The Shirley Plantation facts for this story were obtained by reading the marvelous book by historian Julian Charity, "Courage at Home and Abroad: The Military History of Shirley Plantation." This book was published in 2012 and is available for purchase from the Museum Store at Shirley. Julian was also interviewed and supplied information not fully documented in the book. The facts and tidbits of Shirley's history during 1862-1863 that I received from Julian were invaluable and I pray they enhance the reader's enjoyment of the story.

1)   On a sad note, many of the deceased soldiers' remains were not returned home until after the war. One method of marking the bodies was to stitch the names of the dead inside their coats. The practice of identification varied from place to place. But with my character being a seamstress, I had her embroider with something she believed would last and would contrast inside the dark lining of the jackets. I also sew and have some lovely gold metallic thread that has held

up for years. Hence, I had Angelina use gold for her stitchery.

2)   This is historical fiction and a romance and so some creative license was used for plot purposes. For instance, the real-life Hilly Carter did not die in the time frame portrayed, but later. He was brought home to Shirley by one of his brothers, across Union lines. Matthew and Angelina are fictional characters. They did not assist in freeing Hill Carter who was, with his physician son, held by General Benjamin Butler at a later date than in this story. Mr. and Dr. Carter were eventually returned to their home.

3)   I was inspired to write this story by the wonderful tour guides at the plantation, Lee Hayes in particular. She and Julian brought to life the story of the Shirley women coming out to find Union soldiers encamped in their field. The Carter women served them in Christian charity and were subsequently afforded protection by General McClellan.

4)   The Civil War Yahoo group provided me with the information about advertisements placed in newspapers whereby family members could send messages. This practice ceased, however, later in the war when it was suspected that secret coded messages were being passed in the classifieds.

5)   Another great source of information about Shirley Plantation is *Shirley Plantation:*

Home to a Family and a Business for 11 Generations (2010) by Elinor Warren.

6)　　Clement Vallandigham was a real life Ohio congressman who was arrested and tried by the Union army and later turned over to the Confederate army. Some facts are stranger than fiction! Matthew's congressman father is fictitious and is "friends" with Congressman Vallandigham, a fellow Copperhead.

7)　　J.W. Booth might be construed as John Wilkes Booth in our story but I don't spell that out for the reader. It was fun to imply that my fictional thespian Booth was responsible for some of the evil that happened in the story.

8)　　On the night the real life John Wilkes Booth was in the theater in DC, the show playing there was "Our American Cousin." I didn't know until after I'd chosen that as Matthew's play that it was the actual drama showing the night Lincoln was killed.

Acknowledgements

Julian Charity, historian of Shirley Plantation in Charles City, Virginia, was invaluable to me in establishing the backdrop of real-life Shirley Plantation during the Civil War. Randy Carter, former director Janet Appel, and the staff of Shirley offered such assistance and hospitality. I especially appreciate this trio reading the novella to ensure accuracy.

Kudos also for help on this novella to Kathy Maher, my critique partner for this project, whose quick turn-around on the critiques, knowledge, and ability to brainstorm Civil War ideas were critical to this novella being completed.

Thank you to Julie Lessman, Lisa Norato, and Jocelyn Green for their endorsements! Thanks to my beta readers Debbie Mitchell, Anne Payne, Marian Baay, Diana Flowers, Teresa Matthews, and Noela Nancarrow.

Last, but not least, to my husband and son who have given up wife and mommy time so this project could be completed and our daughter who has been such an encouragement. God has been so good to me.

Thank you all for your help and I thank God that He put you all in my life!

Thank you for reading Return to Shirley Plantation: A Civil War Romance! If you enjoyed it, would you please consider posting a review?

You can connect with me online on Facebook, Pinterest, goodreads, LinkedIn, and Twitter! I also have two group blogs – Overcoming With God and Colonial Quills. Website: www.CarrieFancettPagels.com.

Other books/stories by Carrie Fancett Pagels:

Saving the Marquise's Granddaughter (White Rose/Pelican, ebook June 2016, paperback July 2016)

"Requilted with Love" by Carrie Fancett Pagels in *The Blue Ribbon Brides* Collection (Barbour Books, November, 2016)

The Steeplechase (Forget-Me-Not Romances, February, 2016).

The Substitute Bride (October, 2015), a novella set in Shepherd Michigan and part of the O' Little Town of Christmas collection.

The Christy Lumber Camp Series: *The Fruitcake Challenge* (September, 2014) a Selah Award finalist, *The Lumberjacks' Ball* (April, 2015) and *Lilacs for Juliana* (August, 2015). ALL three books were long list finalists for Family Fiction's novel of the year.

Also, look for: "Snowed In" Carrie's short story published in *A Cup of Christmas Cheer* (Guidepost Books, October, 2013). Available through Guidepost Books website.

Carrie contributed to *God's Provision in Tough Times* by Cynthia Howerter and LaTan Murphy (Lighthouse of the Carolinas, 2013).

Carrie's award winning story "The Quilting Contest" is published in Family Fiction's *The Story* anthology.

Watch for other upcoming publications!

Thank you for reading!!!